STOP AND STARE

KATIA ROSE

Iz

"Should we poke it with something?"

Paulina's fingers dig into my shoulders where she's trying to hide all six foot one of herself behind me. She's whispering like the raccoon might lunge at us with its fangs bared at any minute.

"Maybe we should throw a rock," I answer.

"No! Don't throw a rock at it!" She raises her voice and then yelps and goes back to whispering when the raccoon pauses the little feast he's having and looks at us. "He's too cute."

"If he's cute, why are you hiding behind me?"

"Because he might have rabies!"

I'm not an expert, but I don't think the pudgy raccoon chilling on our house's front steps is showing any signs of rabies. He's propped on his back feet as he munches his way through the contents of a shredded trash bag. He seems to have dragged it out of the knocked-over garbage bin lying next to me and Paulina on the sidewalk.

"Well I'm glad to know you're okay with me getting rabies before you."

"I have longer legs!" she protests. "If you get bit first, I can get help faster."

I burst out laughing at all the ways that doesn't make sense, which makes the raccoon look at us again, which makes Paulina scream, which makes me laugh even more as I shift around under her death grip and pull my phone out of my jacket pocket.

"What are you doing?" she asks.

"Calling Jane." I dial the number of one of our other two housemates and press the phone to my ear. "If she's in the house, maybe she can bang some pots and pans or something and scare it."

Paulina and I have been standing here in the freezing February weather for at least ten minutes. We found the front door blocked by our furry visitor after walking home from campus together. The raccoon hasn't responded to clapping, yelling, or stomping. The only thing it's done besides eat is hiss at us whenever we try to get any closer.

"Yo Jane," I say when the call connects, "you in the Babe Cave?"

It's our official name for the cramped and creaky little row house we rent a few blocks away from the UNS campus—so official we even have it printed on the welcome mat the raccoon is currently using as a dinner table.

"I am. Why?" she asks.

"Because there's a giant, super cute raccoon blocking the door, and it wants to kill us!" Paulina shouts beside my ear.

I wince. "Yeah. That."

"JUMPING JESUS!" Jane bellows, making me wince again. Her Nova Scotian accent roars to life like it always does when she gets angry.

Our fourth roommate, Hope, always says Jane has the

2

spirit of a little old fisherman's wife trapped inside her twenty year-old body, and I kind of believe it. I don't know any other person in their twenties who says things like 'Jumping Jesus,' but then again, Jane is the only east coast native in our friend group. The rest of us are transplants who came to Halifax for university.

"I knew we had raccoons! I just knew it!" she continues. "I knew those little buggers would go after the garbage. We're going to have to secure the bin."

"Uh, right, yeah, but in the meantime, do you have any suggestions? We're kind of stuck outside."

I can feel the tips of my ears going numb. I started growing out my shaved head a few months ago, but my shaggy little excuse for a pixie cut isn't enough to give me any warmth.

"Oh I have many suggestions for that little bugger," Jane mutters in a voice so menacing it almost makes me gulp before she ends the call.

A second later, the door swings back to reveal Jane in a pair of sweatpants with a faded red UNS v-neck on top. Her brown hair is falling out of a messy bun on the very top of her head, her eyes blazing with vengeance as she glares down at the raccoon with a broom clutched in her hands.

I can see the whole 'angry fisherman's wife' thing in moments like this.

"*Git!*" she hollers, stepping forward until her slipper-clad feet are just a few inches from the raccoon. "Git away now! Shoo! Go on! *Git*, you little bugger! Look at this mess you made!"

The raccoon shuffles away from her but doesn't leave the steps. It's clutching an empty pudding cup, and it looks straight at Jane as it slowly licks a clump of congealed chocolate off the plastic.

Jane sucks in a breath and narrows her eyes. "How dare you! This is my home! You have no business darkening my door with your insolence."

She uses the broom to try scooting the raccoon off the steps. It drops the pudding cup and turns to hiss at her. Paulina's fingers dig into my shoulders so tight I'm going to end up with bruises, and even I can feel my blood pressure rising as the raccoon tenses up like it's about to spring.

Instead of moving away, Jane drops into a crouch. My mouth falls open when she twists her face into a sneer and hisses right back.

The raccoon scrambles off the steps and lopes along the sidewalk before disappearing into a gap between two houses down the road.

Jane straightens up, brushes off her sweatpants, and beams at us. "Hey, guys!"

I blink at her. I'm sure Paulina is doing the same thing behind me.

Jane uses the broom to beckon us forward. "Well, come on in!"

"Uh, Jane," I say as I start making my way up the snow-dusted path through the little patch of dead grass we call a front lawn, "did you just *hiss* at a raccoon?"

She shrugs. "If I know anything about raccoons, it's that you've got to show them who's boss."

"You scare me sometimes, Jane," Paulina says as I reach the bottom of the steps. "In a good way. Usually."

She shrugs again. "I'll take that. Now let's get this trash cleaned up before he brings his little friends back with him."

By the time we get everything sorted out and prop a brick on top of the garbage bin to keep anything from scrambling inside, my ears are stinging and my fingers are going numb. I rub my hands together as I step inside and kick off my shoes. Jane has one of her candles going, making the whole house smell like vanilla and something spicy I can't place.

"What's the candle of the day, Jane?" I ask as she heads to the living room and flops down on the worn out, royal blue couch she has covered in textbooks, papers, and a dozen highlighters in a rainbow of colours.

"Vanilla bourbon," she answers in a dreamy voice, pausing to take a huge inhale and close her eyes as she smiles to herself.

Jane really likes candles.

"Do we have actual bourbon?" Paulina asks, stepping past me to claim an armchair. She sits sideways and drapes her model-length legs over one of the edges before running a hand through her long blonde hair. "I could use a drink."

There was a very brief time when I thought I might have a crush on Paulina back in first year. She's pretty enough to be some kind of Polish beauty queen, but she's also a complete dork in the cutest way possible. She's always tripping over stuff, and she has a knack for picking up hobbies she's not actually good at it but stays devoted to nonetheless. The collection of pots and planters coated with snow in our yard are a remnant of her annual failed attempt to grow vegetables.

I realized pretty fast that crushing on Paulina was pointless and that all we had were friendship vibes anyway. She, Jane, Hope, and I are all on the UNS lacrosse team, and the four of us got really close during first year. That combined with the team's 'don't date your teammates' code was enough to make me set my sights on other horizons.

The code wasn't enough to stop the sparks from flying between Hope and our former team captain, Becca. The drama of the century unfolded over the course of the lacrosse season last semester, and the two of them are campus's cutest couple now.

"Is Hope home?" I ask.

Jane nods and glances up at the ceiling. "Her and Becca are *watching a movie.*"

Right on cue, the rhythmic thumping of a headboard against the wall filters down from the second floor.

Paulina laughs. "They always think they're sooooo quiet."

I chuckle too. "*Dios mío.* I have to go up to my room now. I always feel like I have to be extra loud and, like, make my presence known to them, or else I don't know what I'll end up hearing."

"Good luck with that, Izzo," Jane says.

I give the two of them a salute and turn to head up there. The stairs help me out by firing off their usual series of deafening creaks as I get to the second floor. I hear some giggling and shushing coming from Hope's room as I walk up the hallway to mine.

It's past five and dark enough now that I reach for my light switch. The overhead lamp highlights how badly I need to tidy up. Textbooks are stacked in piles on the floor, desk, and bedside table, and clothes are spilling out of my laundry bin like a waterfall of button-downs and UNS sweaters. The walls are covered in a random selection of lacrosse team photos, pride flags, and the paintings and knickknacks from Colombia my dad always gets me on his trips back home.

The only part of the room that actually looks organized is the shoe rack under the window housing my collection of Jordans. My friends always make fun of me for being a lacrosse player who collects basketball shoes, but they just don't understand the glory and thrill of slipping a sick pair of vintage Jordans out of the box and trying them on.

I don't even *wear* some of the shoes; they're too divine to touch the humble soil of the earth. The rack has one shelf for Outside Shoes and one shelf for what I call Trophy Shoes—another thing my friends love to make fun of.

"But we don't need them," I whisper to the Jordans, smiling to myself like I always do when I gaze upon their multi-hued majesty. "They are not worthy of you anyway."

I might be a little obsessed.

After dropping my book-filled Jansport onto the floor next to a basket of laundry I've been meaning to put away for a week, I grab my laptop off my desk and settle onto my bed to get ready for my weekly video call with my best friend Marina.

I have about five minutes to spare, so I slip some headphones on and blast a little Kendrick, sinking into the sound and letting the day of lectures and note-taking roll off me. Even though I'm always busier during the first semester of the year when I'm balancing schoolwork and the lacrosse season, second semester seems to hit harder without the distraction of focusing on the Lobsters.

Apparently the founders of our school decided naming a coastal city's team after the mighty king of crustaceans was cool and not ridiculously stereotypical.

My professors weren't lying when they said third year was going to be tough. It's almost been enough to make me question why I decided to major in something as intense as chemistry—almost. I love chemistry even more than I love all the pick-up lines I get from being a chem major.

Let me tell you something about chemists. We like to do it on the table, periodically.

7

They're never *good* pick-up lines, but they're surprisingly effective.

The *beep beep* sound of an incoming call filters through my headphones, interrupting Kendrick's lyrical genius, which is way more sophisticated than my pick-up lines. I pause the song and press the accept button. Marina's face fills my laptop screen a second later.

She beams at me, just like she always does when we start our calls. Marina has the prettiest damn smile in the world, and seeing her freckled face and big brown eyes feels like home. I could pick her out of any smile line-up in the world. That cute little gap between her front teeth is a dead giveaway.

"Hey, bestie," she greets me.

"Hey, bestie," I answer, shifting so I can lay on my side to face the camera. "How's it going?"

She sighs and flops backward on her couch, holding her phone above her face. Her long brown hair fans out around her like a halo. "It's going. Is it just me, or is third year turning out to be one giant kick in the ass?"

"I was just thinking the same thing. My chem courses are turning the fuck up this year."

"Poli sci isn't any better. Now I actually look forward to writing three thousand word essays about movies for my minor. It's like a soothing break. Isn't that crazy?"

I shake my head and laugh. "You're the only person I know who would find a three thousand word film studies essay soothing."

"Sometimes it's nice to think about stories instead of diplomacy and governance."

I make my eyebrows jump up and down. "You mean it's nice to look at Audrey Hepburn."

Marina's lifelong obsession with Audey Hepburn is legendary. She's seen every single Audrey Hepburn film at least four times, and she's probably watched her favourite, *Roman Holiday*, enough to break world records. Even her phone background is a picture of Audrey Hepburn, although her lock screen is reserved for a photo of the two of us.

It's been the same one for years: an old timey, throw-away camera shot of me and Marina as kids with eyes turned demonically red by the glare. We're sitting in a laundry basket for reasons totally unknown. Marina is wearing a green turtleneck, and I'm behind her in a base-ball cap with my arms wrapped around her and my cheek pressed to hers. Our faces are blurry from laughing so hard.

"We're studying the turn of the millennium!" she protests. "We just watched *The Matrix*."

"And did you sit there picturing Audrey Hepburn in a black leather trench coat?"

She wrinkles her nose and glares at me. "Do not mock Miss Audrey Hepburn. It is her god-given right to be placed on a pedestal by all of human kind. You need to respect that."

"Next thing I know you're going to be telling me Audrey Hepburn was some kind of prophet."

"I mean, if you think about it, she was kind of—"

She cuts herself off to glare at me again when I start laughing so hard I snort.

"I see you cannot take this conversation seriously. I won't say any more." She sits up and makes a show of inspecting the nails of her free hand.

I do my best to stop chuckling. "Aww, come on Marina. You know you're just too cute to handle when you're talking about *Miss* Audrey Hepburn. I love it."

She glances up from her nails, and something flashes in her eyes. My heart starts slamming against my chest in a frantic rhythm, and for a few seconds, I can't do anything except lay there blinking at her while I try to remember how to breathe.

Shit shit shit.

This has been happening more and more lately: the silence after a flirty comment I only meant as a joke. I don't know exactly when these awkward moments started, but I didn't make things any better by deciding to be the *perfecto idiota* of the century on New Year's Eve.

We were both back in Toronto for the holidays, and we decided to go to a friend of a friend's house party together. We didn't know anyone else there, but it didn't matter. We had the time of our lives downing champagne and dancing like the weirdos we are while everyone wondered what the hell we were doing there. She just looked so fucking *pretty* in her black lacy shirt and jeans with sparkly makeup glittering around her eyes. She looked more than pretty; she looked *hot*.

The more I thought about it, the more champagne I drank to try and *stop* thinking about it, but of course that plan backfired.

And then midnight hit.

It was one sloppy, drunken peck on the lips I spent the rest of the night apologizing for, but even now, I'm way too aware of Marina's bottom lip dropping open as she stares at me. I want to bite it. I want to pull my best friend's bottom lip between my teeth and thread my hands into her hair.

It's fucked up. All of it is so fucked up, and I promised myself I'd stop. I promised myself I'd be more careful. There's a place for Marina in my life, and that place is not under me.

No matter how good it feels to think about that.

Mierda.

I shake my head to clear away the pictures taking shape. It's like there's a fog drifting into my brain, obscuring what Marina means to me and turning her into something else, something soft and hot and hungry for me.

Something dangerous.

Marina has always been my safe place. I've always been hers. I don't want any danger here. I don't exactly have the best track record with things working out between me and the girls I'm into. Marina is supposed to be the person I can count on to be there when things go wrong, not the person things go wrong *with*.

"Iz?"

My head is spinning so much the screen in front of me has gone out of focus. I fix my attention on Marina again. She still staring at me with her mouth open just a bit, her eyes wide and searching.

"Sorry. Uh, just tired," I say after giving my head a final shake. My voice comes out all hoarse, and I have to clear my throat. "So many classes today."

"Right. Yeah." She glances down at her bedspread for a second and then back at me.

Double *mierda*.

She's gotta be pissed. She probably thinks I'm coming onto her. It doesn't help that she's sitting there in a v-neck shirt that shows off the perfect sliver of cleavage. She really does have the most amazing, curvy body. It's meant so much to see her discover that too, especially after how hard she was on herself in high school.

"So, um, how were your classes?" she asks.

"Uh..." I try to pull myself back to the present and scan my brain for any traces of how the day went. It's a struggle. "Well, uh...oh! Actually something good happened. One of my profs got my pronouns right!"

Her whole face lights up as she grins at me, and all the

tension fades for a moment. We're back to what we've always been: two friends who look out for each other no matter what.

This is how it's supposed to be, and I really need to get a handle on the part of my brain that's trying harder and harder to fuck it up.

"Iz, that's amazing! I'm so happy for you."

I grin right back at her. "Yeah, I was so shocked. I didn't think he'd remember. Most of them never do. He was going around talking to all the groups in the lab, and when he said something about me to our group, he called me they!"

Marina does a fist pump. "Hooray for they!"

I laugh and join in the fist pumping. "It felt really good. Honestly, I feel like the longer my hair gets, the harder I have to work to like, prove I'm non-binary or something. It's like if I'm not glaringly androgynous, it doesn't count for people."

Marina nods. "That's really shitty. People are so obsessed with gendering everything. I swear, if you put a long blonde wig on top of a lamp, everyone would be like, 'Ah yes, it is a sexy girl lamp now.' It's crazy."

I burst out laughing. "Okay, sexy girl lamp is definitely going to be my next Halloween costume."

Marina doubles over, the phone shaking in her hand as she cackles. "I need to see that. If we were doing a costume party for your birthday, I would demand you do it then."

"That would be a very memorable way to turn twenty-one." I nod like I'm considering it. "By the way, what are you guys doing for my birthday?"

Marina is coming to visit for the occasion next week. She and my roommates have been doing an annoyingly good job of keeping the 'secret theme' of the party they're planning a mystery to me.

Marina winks, and I do my best to ignore the way it makes my pulse kick up again as she speaks in a teasing tone. "Now, now, Iz, you know I can't tell you that."

"Come onnnn," I whine. "I promised to show up at the airport with your favourite Davy Jones pizza. I can retract that promise."

She shakes her head and grins. "Nah, you love me too much for that."

I raise an eyebrow to challenge her but give up after a couple seconds.

"Ugh, you're right. I do."

That's the thing: I do love her. I love her more than anyone, and I'd be an idiot to let myself lose that.

2

Marina

"What are you smiling about?"

My roommate, Alexis, throws a look at me as she heads through the living room on her way to get a snack in the kitchen. I've just put down my phone after ending my weekly call with Iz, and her question makes me realize I'm still grinning at the black screen like Iz's face is going to pop up any second and add in one last joke.

"I was just talking to Iz," I answer. I move my phone from the couch to the coffee table and pick up the cross-stitch I was working on before the call.

"Of courseeeee," Alexis drawls around the mouthful of chips she's just shoved in her face while standing in front of the open cupboard, contemplating her other food options.

She's clearly settled in for the night, with her famous raggedy bunny slippers on under her sweatpants and an equally raggedy white crop top with the words 'Band Geek' printed on it in peeling purple letters.

We're not exactly a 'party hard' kind of house. Most nights, we can be found doing exactly this: me sitting on the couch doing a cross stitch with Netflix on and Alexis wandering out of her room in search of food after a long session of oboe practice. Sometimes we even get really wild and watch an Audrey Hepburn movie together while splitting a bottle of wine.

"You tell them you're in love with them yet?"

I almost drop my needle in the middle of threading it through the next square in my embroidery hoop. "*Alexis!*"

"What?" She wanders over with the chip bag in hand, the giant pile of brown curls pulled into a messy bun on top of her head bouncing as she plops down on the couch next to me. "You *are* going to tell them, right?"

Alexis is one of the most direct people I know, which comes in handy sometimes, but also makes sharing secrets with her an extreme risk. I wouldn't have told her about New Year's Eve if I had anyone else to tell, but seeing as my go-to sounding board for any kind of confession— AKA Iz—was the reason *for* that confession, I ended up going into a rambling story about the kiss during one of Alexis and I's wine and Audrey nights a few weeks ago.

It only took about one sentence from me for her to declare she always knew I was in love with Iz. I didn't even use the word 'love' myself, but she's been ordering me to march up to Iz and tell them ever since. I had to pry my laptop out of her hands to keep her from buying me a plane ticket that very night.

Hence the extreme risk of telling her any secrets.

"No, Alexis, I'm not going to call up my best friend of almost twenty years and say I'm in love with them with absolutely no warning, especially when I'm not even sure that's how I feel, and *extra* especially when I have no idea if that's how they feel."

She rolls her eyes and points at the hoop in my hands, coming dangerously close to sprinkling chip dust on the white fabric. "Marina, level with me here. You are literally *embroidering a picture of the two of you holding hands.* You're in love, girl."

I pause and look at the blocked out design I'm only a few rows away from finishing. I'm not great at making my own cross-stitch patterns, but I'm proud of how this one turned out. It's at least discernibly me and Iz, their red button-down and matching Jordans a contrast to the green sundress I'm wearing. It's based on a photo of us from a couple summers ago. I still need to do the threaded details like the shoelaces and facial expressions, and then the whole thing will come to life.

"What?" I demand. "It's their birthday present. It's cute. Friends make each other stuff like this."

Alexis raises her eyebrows and downs another handful of chips, not even bothering to argue.

I can't blame her. If I'm honest with myself, I can admit this cross stitch is the gayest thing I've ever seen in my life.

If I'm even more honest with myself, I can admit there's no way Iz and I are just friends anymore—or at least, they're not just a friend to me.

Being with Iz feels like being myself. We just fit. When we're together, I feel like I'm wrapped up in my favourite blanket, the one that's worn and soft in all the right places and always smells like warm laundry.

That's what loving someone is supposed to feel like. I've dated a bit since I started college, but it always comes back to that: nobody feels like Iz. Nobody makes me feel that same crazy combination of safe and electrified that zings through me every time they look at me a certain way.

That's the thing: I *know* they look at me a certain way. I've seen it happen again and again. Ever since we left high school, there have been these *moments* during our visits and our calls where things between us shift. The silence stretches on a little too long. We get caught up in each other's eyes and then look away, both of us breathing hard. The looming sensation that *something* is about to happen hangs so thick in the air it gets hard to breathe at all.

But nothing ever does happen. It's always the same, just like tonight on the call when they called me cute. I know friends call each other cute all the time. We've been calling each other cute since we were kids, but *just* friends don't go quiet and stare at each other the way we did after that.

I felt it then: the weight of *something* hanging between us. I was so sure of it I couldn't move. I couldn't force out the words I wanted to say.

Do you really think I'm cute, Iz?

I don't know what they would have said, but I needed to find out. It's become clearer and clearer there's something here besides friendship.

Of course that scared me when I realized it. Of course it kept me up at night. Of course it made me feel crazy and terrified of putting one of the most important things in my life at risk, but when Iz leaned in at midnight during the New Year's Eve party we went to in Toronto a few weeks ago, it finally clicked: not going after this—whatever *this* is—would be even scarier than risking it all.

Just one sloppy, champagne-fueled peck on the lips made the whole night explode into shimmering shades of colour I'd never seen before. Iz went bright red and apologized a second later, but I didn't want an apology.

I wanted more.

Alexis keeps sitting there crunching on her chips like the embodiment of the sassiest side of my subconscious, and after completing a few more squares of the cross-stitch, I give in and sigh.

"Look, even if I *was* completely ready to tell Iz, I couldn't. They'd freak the fuck out."

"Um, I don't think so." Alexis shakes her head. "I've seen you guys together when they've visited here. They're clearly head over heels for you."

My pulse picks up at the thought of it, and I'm glad Alexis can't hear the way my heart is clanging against my ribcage.

"Even if that were true, it's...it's not that simple."

"What's not simple about it?" She shrugs. "Seems pretty simple to me. You like each other, so tell each other."

Now it's me shaking my head. "Iz...has a hard time trusting other people's feelings. They have a hard time trusting their own feelings. I don't think it would ever be a matter of just telling each other and taking it from there."

I know that better than anyone. I was there for Iz through their first heartbreak. I've been there for them through every heartbreak since. If the thought of letting our friendship shift into something more makes me nervous, that's nothing compared to the utter terror I can imagine Iz feeling.

"So, what, you're gonna bottle it all up forever because it might be hard for them? Is that fair to *you*?"

"I..." The needle goes still in my hands again, halfway through finishing the final corner of one of Iz's shoes. "Look, this is all still so new for me. I only started seriously thinking about it as a possibility at New Year's. We're talking about the person I've been best friends with since we were toddlers. Can we just leave it at that for tonight?"

"Of course, yeah." She sets the chip bag down on the table and spreads her hands in surrender. "Sorry if I pushed too hard on this. You know I just want to see you happy."

"Hmm." I glance over at the TV sitting on a cheap IKEA stand across the room. "You know what would make me happy?"

"What?"

"If you went and put on *Roman Holiday* for us to watch."

She drops her head back and groans. "Seriously? *Roman Holiday* again? How many times have you seen that movie?"

"It's my favourite!" I protest. "And you said you wanted to make me happy."

"Ugh, fine." She keeps grumbling to herself as she heads over to get my favourite Audrey Hepburn movie of all time going.

It's my favourite movie of all time, period. I've stopped counting how many times I've seen it, and I still manage to find something new to love every time I watch Miss Audrey zip around Rome on a moped as the runaway Princess Ann.

When we were kids, Iz and I used to play our own make-believe version of the movie all the time. I'd be Princess Ann, of course, and Iz would pull me around the yard in a wagon that was supposed to be our getaway vehicle. We'd imagine there were paparazzi and royal officials hiding out in the bushes trying to catch us, and we'd wedge the wagon behind the shed in my parent's yard to get 'undercover.' Sometimes we'd sit back there for hours, sharing snacks we'd packed beforehand and talking about what an amazing life we could have together in Rome if we managed to escape.

"Hey, Marina," Alexis says after settling herself back on the couch once the opening credits begin to play, "I know I'm already pushing it, but just...maybe when you're in Halifax for Iz's birthday—"

"*Alexis,*" I warn.

"Okay, okay." She waves her hands in the air. "Like I said, I just want to see you happy."

I watch the black and white images of 1950s Rome on the screen, still thinking about Iz and I in that wagon, their hand in mine as they dropped their squeaky kid's voice into a fake baritone and told me they'd show me the world, and I nod.

I just want to see us happy too.

3

Marina

There's one part of flying that always makes me feel like I'm going to puke. I'm fine for the takeoff. I'm fine for the landing. I'm fine for the part where we're cruising through the air. Not even turbulence sets off my stomach, but if I look out the window and see the plane is turning and doing that tilty thing where the ground is at a crazy angle and the sky has gone sideways, I start dry-heaving right on cue.

The lady next to me refused to switch and take the window seat, even after I told her I'm not great with flying. I can see her out of the corner of my eye, leaning forward so she can stare past me and out the round little window giving us a view of the sickening funhouse trip outside.

If you wanted to look out the window, why the hell wouldn't you sit next to it?

I bite my lip to keep from asking out loud and start rubbing little circles onto my stomach in an attempt to calm it down.

Almost there. Almost there, and then you'll see Iz.

I picture them standing in the arrivals area, and I feel the corners of my mouth lift. I haven't seen Iz in person since New Year's. We've gone way longer without a visit during our years of university, but that doesn't make it any easier to spend time apart from the person I grew up seeing nearly every day.

The fact that we kissed the last time I saw them and haven't talked about it since is, however, adding a few flips to my stomach's routine.

"Attendants, please..."

The rest of what the captain says over the speakers is too garbled for me to make out over the supposed-to-be-soothing nature sounds I have streaming through my head-phones, but I look to the front of the plane and see the two flight attendants strapping themselves into their pull-down seats.

I risk a glance out the window and see the plane is parallel with the ground again. My shoulders unclench, and I sag against my seat. My stomach does one final somersault and then relaxes into merciful stillness. I pull my headphones out of my ears and watch Nova Scotia get closer and closer beneath us.

Everything is coated in white like a fine sugar dusting, and the sky is a silvery grey. We pass over streets lined with homes that look like tiny dollhouses from up here. They get bigger and bigger until we're finally zooming over the airport and gliding down onto the tarmac.

The plane is small enough that the landing makes my teeth chatter as I'm jostled around in my seat, but now that we're no longer in danger of the horizon shifting at vomit-inducing angles, my stomach is only tightening with excitement.

No matter what else we have going on, I'll always be eager for that first hug from Iz. I whip my seatbelt off as soon as the little light telling us to wear them switches off. I pull my shoulder bag out from under the seat in front of me and wiggle into my coat, doing my best not to smack the lady next to me in the face with my flailing arms, even if part of me thinks she deserves it. Then I sit there bouncing my heels up and down as I wait for the plane to empty.

I'm almost excited enough I don't feel the familiar wave of apprehension hit as I get into the aisle and reach up to grab my suitcase—almost.

I can still hear those old jeering voices in my head telling me everyone is watching and laughing at the fat girl filling the aisle. I resist the urge to tug my shirt down where it's creeping up over the edge of my jeans and focus on getting a hold of my bag's handle.

You are allowed to be here. There's nothing wrong with you.

I repeat my mantra in my head as I start wheeling the bag up the aisle. I used to try telling myself no one was laughing or staring, but that didn't work out so great on the occasions when I'd look around and find people *were* laughing or staring.

The truth is, there'll always be someone ready to get offended by the size of my thighs or the roll of skin that forms over the waistband of pretty much every pair of pants I own, since most companies are still bad at making comfy jeans for curvy girls. If I focus on what other people think, I'm always going to find a reason to feel bad, so now I focus on myself. Sometimes it works and sometimes it doesn't, but most days, I'm pretty damn proud to be me.

I wave to the flight attendants and say thank you as I pass by. The Halifax airport is tiny, and it only takes me a couple minutes of speed-walking before I'm at the door to the arrivals area. I burst through and find it busier than I expected. My first scan of the people standing around in puffy winter coats and snow boots doesn't bring any sign of Iz, but as I'm wheeling my suitcase over to a bench and pulling out my phone to text them, I hear that familiar voice calling my name.

"Yo, Mariiiiiina!"

They sing it out loud enough to make a few heads turn, rolling the *r* just like their dad always does. A second later, Iz clears the crowd, and a smile so big it makes my cheeks ache takes over my face.

They're wearing an oversized green army jacket over one of those crazy button-downs they're always finding in the dollar bin at the thrift store. This one is dark blue with a pattern of tiny oranges that matches their citrus-coloured Jordans.

I wouldn't exactly call Iz on-trend, but they always manage to look very fucking stylish.

Their hair is in the fluffy, haphazard stage of growing out a buzz cut, and the length has a cute puppy dog effect. I can't help reaching up to ruffle it as they charge the few feet of distance left between us and fling themself into my arms.

"You're so fluffy!" I say as I pull them closer.

The two of us laugh and stand there wrapped up in each other, swaying to the generic lobby music pumping through the speakers. I take a deep breath in and let out a humming sigh. Iz makes the same sound.

"I'm soooo happy you're here!" they gush. "How has it only been a month and a half? I feel like I haven't seen you in so long."

"You're right." I drop my hands to their shoulders and step back. "Let me gaze upon your glorious face."

They do an exaggerated fashion model pout and twist their head around so I can see all the angles. I laugh and call them a dumby dumb dumb—our favourite made-up insult from when we were kids—but even as I grab my suitcase and start following them out of the terminal, I can feel the heat rising in my cheeks.

Iz is hot. I don't know how six weeks made such a difference, but if I thought it was hard to ignore what their little smirk does to me during Christmas break, that's nothing compared to how distracting it is now. My whole body feels warm, and despite the fact that I've ruffled their hair more times than I can count, I can't get over how it felt to have it between my fingers with their body pressed to mine.

The bustle of the airport keeps us quiet until we're outside waiting for a bus into the city. Iz nudges a pebble along the pavement with the toe of their shoe before looking up to speak to me.

"Sorry about your pizza. The delivery guy didn't come in time, but it will be waiting when we get there, if my roommates don't eat it all first."

I blink. "Pizza?"

The concept rings a bell, but I'm still too busy recovering from the hug-induced haze to remember why I'm supposed to want pizza.

Iz chuckles and does that smirk again. It does not help with the haze-clearing.

"Remember?" they prompt. "I was supposed to bring you pizza when I picked you up. You specifically requested the chicken option from Halifax's most finest purveyor of cheesy delights: Davy Jones Pizza."

I blink again. "Ohhhh right. Wow, yeah, you really dropped the ball, Iz. I should turn around and get on a flight back right now."

I try to hide how much my head is spinning by making a show out of pretending to be offended. I turn to face the doors behind us and flick my hair over my shoulder before starting to wheel my suitcase away. Iz is laughing at me, and the sound almost cracks my fake glare to make me laugh too. I keep the charade going, and I'm about to reach for the door when I feel their hand clamp around my wrist.

My breath catches in my throat. Iz starts to say something teasing, but when I look back over my shoulder at them, their voice trails off into silence. I see their eyes get wide, and I *know* I'm not imagining it when their gaze drops to my lips for just a second before fixing on their fingers wrapped tight around my arm.

I look down too. The cuff of my jacket leaves just enough of my skin exposed for me to feel the warmth of their hand. The heat blooming from that one point of contact is enough to make my breath catch a second time.

It's like I can already see it playing out: Iz's thumb brushing over the paper-thin skin above my veins, me shivering and saying their name like it's something between a question and permission, the tense second of hesitation before they'd pull me closer, the feeling of their hot breath on my lips just before I'd finally get to find out what they taste like.

Our sloppy peck of a kiss at New Year's didn't give me a chance to do that. I've spent way too many nights since wondering what Iz would taste like, how they'd sound and move. It all feels so wrong and weird and thrilling and right. It's everything all at once, and I can't make any sense of it, but I don't think I want to.

I just want them. I want them to want *me*.

"Iz..."

My voice is so low I doubt they can hear me over the rush of cars and buses pulling up to the airport, but their eyes flick to mine, and they don't drop my hand.

I force myself to take a breath. "Iz, we—"

"That's our ride!"

A bus pulls up to the curb beside us, the brakes squeaking as the door pops open. Iz whips their head around and releases my wrist, facing away from me as they fish around in their pockets for bus tickets.

"I know I have extra ones for you somewhere..." they mumble as they pat down their coat.

Their voice sounds even—too even, like nothing happened at all. They don't look at me until they've found the tickets and stepped up to the bus, and when they glance back my way, they've got that typical Iz grin on.

And I, typically, have to stand there wondering if I imagined everything that just happened.

"You all right?" they ask.

I take a step forward and nod, even though my stomach has started doing flips again. If things between Iz and I keep shifting this quickly, I'm going to spend the whole trip nauseous.

⊏⊐

STOMACH PROBLEMS OR NOT, I can't resist the call of Davy Jones pizza as the scent of gooey cheese, tangy barbeque chicken, and grilled red onion hits my nose. I've already had two giant pieces, but I go in for a third. Davy Jones really is a miracle. I don't know what I'm going to do if Iz moves away after university and I don't have an excuse to come to Halifax anymore.

Hope, one of Iz's housemates, raises the slice she's just taken out of the pepperoni and cheese box and holds it in the air like a substitute champagne flute. "Welcome to the Babe Cave, Marina! Let's do a pizza toast!"

We're crowded into the townhouse's little living room with all of Iz's three housemates. Pizza boxes are covering the whole top of the coffee table, and there's a pop playlist pumping out of a speaker set while the pink string lights in the front window cast a soft glow over us all.

The bond the four of them have going on is so cute it almost makes me jealous. I love living with Alexis, but we don't compare to the way Iz and their friends are all joined at the hip like a gang of besties in some idealized teen movie about what it's like to move away for college. Iz always has some crazy story about what they've all been up to, whether it's pranking their lacrosse team or shutting down a campus bar during one of their legendary nights out.

I rarely do anything more exciting than go to an art house screening with people from my film studies classes, but FOMO aside, I'm happy Iz has these girls. They've been there for them through everything I couldn't be more than a face on a screen for: their coming out as non-binary in second year, all the heartbreaks they've experienced with girls on campus, and the mundane stuff like pulling all-nighters before exams or figuring out class schedules. Iz and I tell each other everything over video, but that only goes so far when you're struggling. It helps to know these girls will always fight for Iz—almost as hard as I will.

"PIZZA TOAST!" Iz shouts, grabbing a fresh slice to hold it up like Hope.

"What exactly is a pizza toast?" I ask, dragging my attention away from the adorable flecks of tomato sauce stuck to Iz's cheek and focusing back on the discussion.

"First you gotta put your pizza in the air," Hope instructs me as she uses her free hand to adjust her glasses.

Hope is one of those girls who always looks effortlessly cool—truly effortlessly, like really did just wake up like that. The ends of her hair are dyed in a teal ombre, a sleeve tattoo covers one of her arms, and even though I've never seen her wear anything except UNS Lobsters merch and sweatpants, she looks like she's just as ready to walk into an underground music festival as she is to show up at lacrosse practice.

I know she's closest with Jane, but when her and Iz get going, they're the wild ones of the group. The three of us went out one time two summers ago and ended up attempting to drunkenly skinny dip in the harbor at three in the morning—or at least, Iz and Hope tried to skinny dip. I stood on the dock and yelled at them while they leaned over the side and splashed me. We very narrowly avoided being caught by the police.

Whatever it is, a pizza toast at least sounds like it won't break any laws.

"Jane! Paulina! You too!" Hope orders. "We are toasting to Marina's safe arrival and to a flawless party for Iz this weekend."

"And the theme is...?" Iz pipes up, doing their best to trick us into spilling the secret.

Hope wags her finger at them. "Nuh-uh. It's a surprise. You'll find out on Saturday."

"But it's Thursday," they whine. "That's so far away."

"How do you say 'too bad' in Spanish?" Hope asks.

"Like this." Iz flips her off. Jane and Paulina burst out laughing while Hope sticks out her tongue.

"Whatever. Let's do this toast. Pizzas up, ladies and distinguished non-binary humans!"

Everyone leans forward to hold their slices in the air over the coffee table.

"To Iz and Marina!" Hope shouts.

Then they all slam their pieces of pizza together.

"Oh my god, no!" I shriek. "No way!"

Iz elbows me from their spot beside me on the couch. "You have to do it, Marina! It's a pizza toast."

"It's good luck!" Jane adds.

Jane is usually the mom-type of the group, and even she's in on this grossness.

"I don't want to waste this delicious pizza," I protest.

They're all still holding their slices together in a gooey mass.

"Oh, you won't waste it," Iz explains. "You have to eat it after. Otherwise it's bad luck."

"You guys are crazy."

"Oh, we know. Now put your pizza up." Iz laughs and pats me on the thigh.

It's just a brief touch, a couple inches above my knee, but it's enough to make me want to squeeze my legs together. I don't want anyone to spot the heat creeping up my neck, so I give in and slap my pizza to the slice pile. I wince as a glob of cheese drops onto the table.

"Atta girl!" Jane woops, her Nova Scotian accent coming out in full force.

"To Iz and Marina!" Hope shouts again, and we all echo the toast.

I glance at Iz as I pull my slice away and nibble a little bite. I am not convinced about this whole pizza toast thing, but I can't ignore how good 'Iz and Marina' sound together.

I just wish I knew Iz heard it too.

4

Iz

My hand is shaking as I bring my toothbrush up to my mouth. My reflection is pale in the chipped, old mirror above our bathroom sink, and even though I'd like to blame the way the room shifts in and out of focus on the beer I had with dinner and the two others I downed while we sat around finishing our pizza and playing Cards Against Humanity, I know I'm not drunk.

I'm just terrified. I tried to keep the game going for as long as possible, but my roommates all dropped off one by one, complaining about early classes tomorrow. I have a lecture at nine in the morning, but I would have sat in the living room all night if it meant avoiding what's about to happen next.

Marina is in my bedroom. In her pajamas. Possibly already in my bed.

My bed where we will be sleeping together tonight.

We grew up sharing beds, air mattresses, and basement floors. I've slept beside her more times than I can count. I've drifted off in the middle of conversations about our dreams and futures. I've shaken her awake when she snores too loud. She's put me in my place when I steal the blankets in my sleep.

Sharing a bed should be normal, but somehow, my throat is so dry from nerves I almost choke on my toothpaste.

"Get it together, Sanchez," I warn my reflection.

I keep *noticing* Marina. Things that should be familiar and easy are suddenly new and hard to navigate: the sound of her laugh, the way she presses her lips together when she's thinking, the sweet smell of her hair when we sit side by side. That look she gave me when I grabbed her arm at the airport nearly killed me.

"She did *not* give you a look." I spit out my toothpaste so I can speak more clearly to myself. "There was no looking. There will be no looking. This is Marina, for fuck's sake."

My best friend Marina. No nice-smelling hair is worth forgetting that.

It does smell *really* nice, though. She must have used some kind of fancy flowery shampoo. I'm not great at identifying flower smells, but I think it might be jasmine.

I grip the edge of the sink as I start to imagine kissing her for about the fourteenth time today.

This is all so fucked up. I don't know what changed or why, but I need to pull it together and find a way to reverse that change. Marina isn't some girl from the campus sports bar. She isn't someone I can watch walk away. That's what happens with the people I date: they walk away. They tell me I'm too much, that I take it too seriously, that college is supposed to be about fun, not falling in love.

I've tried to focus on the fun. I don't have trouble doing that in any other part of my life. I try to keep it casual with the girls I date, but then the feelings start and I get my hopes up only for it to end the same way it always does.

Because I'm too much.

I don't why I didn't learn the first time. I don't know why I keep trying.

Heat pricks the corners of my eyes as I clutch the sink so hard my knuckles go white. I pry my grip off and splash some water on my face, forcing the tears to clear.

This is exactly what's wrong with me. I haven't even made a move on Marina, and I'm already crying. Of fucking course people think I'm too much. Of course they all back away slowly and then run as far as they can. I'm a half-Colombian, gender non-conforming jock with way too many feelings. Of course people don't know what to do with me.

I can't let that happen with Marina. I can't lose her like I've lost so many people before, so I need to stop being an *idiota* about this whole New Year's kiss thing and pull myself together.

I head out into the hall in an old lacrosse t-shirt and some boxers, my clothes from today balled up and pressed to my chest. Our creaky house moans and groans in a familiar pattern as I walk to my room. I open the door and find Marina sitting on the edge of my bed, looking at her phone. She glances up at me, and the yellow glow from my bedside lamp softens her face and catches in her eyes.

She's just so pretty. She's wearing a loose white t-shirt and some fluffy pajama pants, her dark hair hanging down over her shoulders, her skin all soft and dusted with freckles.

"Hey," she says.

"Hey," I answer, forcing myself to snap out of my trance and walk over to the bed. I swallow and nod at her phone. "Did you tell your parents you got in?"

"Uh huh." She finishes typing something out and sets

the phone on my bedside table. "They say to send you their love."

"You know what I wish they'd send me?" I say as I keep myself busy with putting my clothes away and clearing some of the random crap off the floor. I cleaned two days before Marina got here, but I've already gone back to my leaving-stuff-on-the-floor ways.

"What?"

"A milkshake. Your mom makes the best milkshakes ever. Do you remember those boujee ones she used to make when we were kids? They had all those toppings. It was like two desserts in one. Oh, and sometimes she'd make those mini banana split ones..."

I glance over my shoulder to find Marina propped up against my headboard, grinning at me. "Yeah, they were so good. I don't know how exactly she would send you one from Toronto, though."

"She could stick it in a cooler and send it via private jet."

Marina snorts. "For you, Iz, I'm sure she would. You know my parents adore you."

"As they should." I toss a few button-downs in the laundry bin. "I'm pretty adorable."

"You really are."

I freeze. She's doing that thing where she presses her lips together while she looks at me, and with her sitting on my bed like that, it would be so easy to walk over and pin her hands above her head. I could lean down and kiss her, *really* kiss her this time.

Calm the fuck down, idiota.

I look away and start tidying like my life depends on it, zipping around the room like a two-legged Roomba on Speed.

"You know you don't have to do that."

I pause when Marina breaks the cleaning-filled silence after a couple minutes. "Do what?"

"Clean up. I'm not, like, a house guest. I'm your best friend. You don't need to impress me."

"Oh, uh..." I put the text book I'm holding back down on the teetering stack on my desk. "Right."

I don't usually clean for her arrival. I'll move enough stuff around to make space for her bags and ensure everything is traversable, but she's right: she's not a regular guest. She's Marina. She knows me, and I know her. Everything is supposed to be simple. It's all supposed to be so much easier than this.

"You okay, Iz?"

"Yeah." I drum my fingers against the glossy book cover. "Yeah, um, I think I'm just tired."

"Oh right, you have class tomorrow morning. We should get to bed."

I really need to take a deep, cleansing breath, but I don't want to freak her out. I settle for running a hand down my face as she gets up and pulls back the blankets.

I didn't think anyone's butt could look sexy in fluffy, mom-style pajama pants, but hers does.

"Which side do you want?"

"Uh, doesn't matter," I answer. "You know me. I like to starfish."

She makes a *pshhh* sound. "Yeah, and subsequently elbow me in the face."

"I'll do my best to keep my hands to myself."

Oh shit.

Oh shit shit shit.

I don't even have a Spanish swear word strong enough for this situation. Marina freezes where she's still getting the blankets sorted, and a few seconds of silence pass during which I wonder if I'm about to pass out.

"We'll see about that," she finally mumbles. "I guess I'll take the far side, then?"

I find enough motor skills to make myself nod. I'm being a creep. Any second now, she's probably going to tell me off for making things so weird.

Instead, she settles herself under the blankets. I hesitate for a moment and then focus enough to drag my feet across the room and drop down onto my side of the bed. I settle my head on the pillow and lay flat on my back, staring up at the ceiling. I know she can probably see how fast my chest is rising and falling under my t-shirt, but I can't move to hide it.

I'm lying down beside her in bed, and it's most definitely a horrible mistake. If I thought I wanted her before, it's nothing compared to what being horizontal beside her is doing to my body.

"Uh, Iz?"

"Yep?" My answer comes out sounding like a wheeze.

"Do you, um, want to turn the light out?"

"Oh. Right. Yeah. Light."

I take another few rapid breaths and then roll onto my side, flailing for the lamp's switch before the room goes dark. My eyes take a few seconds to adjust after I flip onto my back again, but soon I can make out the glow from the streetlamp outside seeping through the UNS flag I use as a curtain.

I still haven't gotten under the blankets. My skin feels too hot for them anyway. Every inch of me is on high alert. I don't know how long we lay there like that. It could be five minutes. It could be a whole hour. I'm not any closer to falling asleep when her whisper cuts through the quiet.

"Iz?"

I swallow. "Yeah?"

"I think we need to talk."

"Oh?"

"Come on." She sighs, and I can practically hear her rolling her eyes. The familiar tone cuts a microscopic amount of the tension. "You know we do."

I chew on my lip for a second. "Okay. Yeah. You're right. We need to talk."

I can't get any farther than that. We're lying still and quiet in the dark, but really we're edging along a tight rope with music of impending doom blasting in the background. We can't stand balanced on the middle of this line forever, but moving seems just as dangerous as staying where we are.

"You know you mean the world to me, right?" Marina begins. "Even going to school so far away from each other didn't change that. Nothing would ever change that, Iz."

But that's where she's wrong. She's already so wrong. If I don't find a way to hide these feelings from her, this will go the way it always does when I like someone.

I'll be too much. I'm always too much.

I shift so I'm not lying there like a corpse anymore and twist my head to face her. I can just make out the curve of her nose and the glint of her eyes in the darkness. "I don't know what I'd do without you."

She chuckles, the sound soft and low. "Well good thing you won't ever have to find out, you dumby dumb dumb."

I breathe out a laugh at our favourite made-up insult from when we were kids, but it's not enough to stop the panic rising in my chest from getting stronger by the second. I clutch the edge of the blankets in my fist.

"I mean it, Marina. You're my person. I'm close with my friends here, but you've known me my whole life. You've been there for everything. Did you know you're the only person I wasn't scared to come out to? Not even a little bit."

She's pansexual, and I'm sure she feels that tiny twinge of terror every time she has to come out to someone new, even someone she trusts. That's how I felt telling my roommates I was non-binary. That's how I felt telling the whole lacrosse team about my new pronouns. No matter how long you've known someone or how well you're sure it's going to go, coming out is always scary.

Except with her. With her, it was as easy as breathing. I didn't feel weird or crazy for saying I realized I'm not a girl *or* a guy. I didn't feel embarrassed to admit that sometimes I like being called handsome but also don't mind the fact that I have boobs. I didn't feel like a freak or a lunatic. I just felt like a person figuring myself out with her by my side.

"I didn't know that." She shifts her head closer to the edge of her pillow. "It means a lot that you wanted to tell me, Iz. I was really honored. I still am."

"You're my person," I repeat. I try to fill those three words with all the things I can't seem to say: the fear, the worry, the hope, the uncertainty, the frustration, the longing, the love.

I love her. I've loved her since we could barely pronounce the word 'love' during our toddler play dates, and we've spent our whole lives since saying that word to each other. Now there's this fucked up *thing* forcing itself between us, making me feel awkward and confused about saying even that. None of it makes sense anymore, and I'm scared. I'm so scared I can barely breathe.

I don't realize I'm shaking until her hand reaches to grip my shoulder and makes me go still. Instead of lighting me up, this time her touch turns me quiet. Some of the thoughts buzzing in my head stop pinging around my brain and let me catch my breath.

"You're my person, Iz," she says once my inhales and

exhales have levelled out. Her hand slides from my shoulder and down to where her fingers can twine with mine. "That's what I want."

I squeeze her hand, and she starts rubbing her thumb over my knuckles. Her touch is so soothing, like a lullaby traced into my skin. I close my eyes and let the smell of jasmine fill my lungs.

Marina.

This is what I want. We don't have to be anything except this. I can forget the rest as long as I get to keep her near me.

She keeps brushing her thumb along the back of my hand, and all the knots in me begin to untie themselves. I shift on the bed, sliding my feet under the blankets. We lay there for so long I can't tell if I've started dreaming.

"Iz?"

Her voice sounds like it's coming from far away, and mine is groggy when I answer.

"Yeah?"

"We're going to be okay. You know that, right?"

My muscles have gone sluggish, and I'm slipping into a dream about jasmine flowers, but I can still pull myself back enough to squeeze her hand.

"I know. We're gonna be okay."

I'll make sure of it. I'll protect this. I'll show her—and myself—I'm not going to do anything stupid or put us at risk. I'll show her she can trust me. I'll show her I can be her person, just like she's always been mine.

5

Marina

I wake up smiling. The outdated popcorn ceiling in Iz's bedroom comes into view, and I grin up at it for a few seconds before I realize what I'm so happy about.

We held hands.

We held hands in this bed last night and talked about being each other's person. We said everything would be all right. I know it's not much, but for the first time, I don't feel crazy for thinking something might be happening between Iz and I.

The air is sharp with possibility, like a bright winter morning when you walk outside and find the world covered in a fresh coat of snow.

A blank canvas.

A story waiting to be told.

It's the cheesiest thing I've ever thought, but it doesn't stop me from rolling over to press the sheets to my nose and catch the lingering scent of Iz's skin. I have a dim memory of them getting up earlier this morning to get ready for class, and I can hear music, voices, and clanging dishes drifting up from the main floor. I scooch over to grab my phone off the bedside table and check the time.

It's just past eight, but the light filtering through the red UNS flag tacked over the window makes it feel much earlier. I stretch in bed and then push myself to my feet.

I head downstairs after digging through my suitcase for a sweater. The steps creaks so loud I'm scared I'm about to puncture the wood. Paulina walks past the end of the stairway and into the narrow entryway, laughing when she looks up and sees me wincing at the sounds of torture the house is making.

"Don't worry about it. They do that all the time."

"I feel like I'm about to break through and fall into the depths of hell."

"That would be an interesting start to Friday morning." She finishes the last bite of toast in her hands and then bends down to pull her boots on. "Any plans for the day? Is Iz ditching to keep you entertained?"

She straightens back up and wiggles her eyebrows at me. I try to play it cool, but I feel my neck get hot and my heart speed up before she tips her head back and laughs.

"Just kidding." She turns to the door and then glances back over her shoulder. "Or am I? Either way, you'll have the house to yourselves. Bye now!"

I blink at the stream of sunlight that pours into my eyes as she yanks the door open. As soon she pulls it shut behind her, I let out a breath I didn't know I was holding.

I didn't think Iz and I were *that* obvious during dinner last night.

Some of my nerves start to come back, squeezing my lungs and twisting my stomach. It can't be good for people to know about this when even Iz and I don't know what *this* is yet.

All we have is a few sentences whispered as we were

falling asleep, a few fragile moments we haven't even talked about yet. I'm hopeful, but I heard the fear in Iz's voice. I know this is still delicate.

I walk into the kitchen and find Hope washing dishes and Iz sitting at the little round table in the corner, shoveling scrambled eggs into their mouth while looking at something on their phone. They glance up when I call out good morning, and the way they beam at me as soon as our eyes lock sends a wave of relief through my body.

"Hey, sleepyhead."

I pretend to be offended. "I didn't get up that much later than you."

"I was talking about the snoring," Iz counters as I grab a seat at the table. "Damn, you were really going."

"I do not snore!"

"Do I need to pull out the famous video evidence I took when we were twelve? I'm sure Hope would enjoy it."

I steal a piece of egg off their plate. "Maybe Hope would enjoy knowing what a starfish you are. Maybe I should take video evidence of you trying to push me off the bed in your sleep."

"I do not do that!"

Hope cuts off our exchange of verbal repartees with a laugh. "Oh my god, you guys are like an old married couple. This is so entertaining."

Once again, I freeze and feel my heart start racing at the implication. I glance at Iz to check for any signs they're freaking out.

If they are, they don't show it in the way they down another mouthful of eggs and then point their fork at Hope. "We're nothing compared to you and Jane. Hanging out with you two in the morning is like being at my grandparents' house, except there's no Colombian music blasting in the background."

Hope chuckles. "Maybe it's a best friend thing. Sometimes best friends act like couples even more than actual couples do. Jane and I are like bickering wives at breakfast, but Becca and I are so chill when we're together in the morning."

"Oh we know you like to *chill*," Iz says, "as in the Netflix and chill definition of chill."

"Maybe that's the key." Hope puts away the pan she's just dried and turns to smirk at us. "Maybe people do less of the old couple bickering thing if they're banging all the time."

Beside me, Iz starts to choke on their eggs.

"Damn Iz, don't die on us!" Hope says as Iz coughs a few times before reaching for the orange juice in front of them and gulping it down.

I don't have the excuse of choking, but I know my cheeks are probably as red as Iz's by now.

"Oh shit," they say after getting themself under control and glancing at the microwave clock. "I'm gonna be late."

They finish up their last bite of eggs and get up from the table without looking at me. Hope offers to wash their dishes, and Iz only turns to me after dropping everything off in the sink. "You can have whatever food you want, Marina, unless it's got someone's name on it. Sorry I have so many classes today. I'll make it up to you at dinner. You're okay to get there yourself?"

I'm still trying to figure out exactly what dynamic we have going on, but I force myself to chuckle.

"We grew up in Toronto, Iz. The entire city of Halifax is the size of our neighbourhood."

Hope smacks the counter. "Bazinga! Spoken like a true crotchety old wife."

I laugh, but Iz's whole mood seems to have shifted.

They barely even look at me as they lift the corners of their mouth in a fake smile.

"Don't worry about class," I tell them, trying to catch their eye. "I have papers to work on all day anyway. I'll see you tonight."

"Cool." They drum their fingers on the counter, hovering for a few seconds before they turn to leave.

I wait for them to come back, to give me *something*, but I hear the front door open a minute later.

What the hell?

Hope is humming along to the song playing on her phone. When the bang of the door closing echoes back to us in the kitchen, she pauses with the dish she's washing still in her hand and turns to me.

"I know it's none of my business, but that seemed...odd. Are you guys fighting or something?"

"Uh..." I watch her go back to grooving around the tiny kitchen, drying cutlery and pulling cupboards open in time with the song. "Not that I know of."

"That just seemed to get randomly tense, so I thought I'd ask. We're all pretty nosy in this house." She flips the dishtowel over her shoulder and gives me an apologetic shrug as she goes back to scrubbing plates in the sink. "Sorry if it was weird of me."

"Not as weird as Iz," I blurt.

Hope looks back at me, head tilted to the side like she's waiting for more, but I squeeze my lips together in an attempt to stay quiet.

She turns to the sink again. "Soooo...believe it or not, I'm actually a pretty good listener. I know it's probably hard to be stuck in this city for four days if something's up with you and Iz, especially since it's their birthday tomorrow. Nothing worse than wanting to yell at someone and not being able to because it's their birthday. I'm just saying, if you need to get it out to someone, I totally get it."

She's leaning against the counter to face me now, and I don't see anything but sincerity in the concerned look she's giving me from behind her glasses.

It hits me then: just how lonely I'm feeling. I've only been here one night, and I've already gone through the full spectrum of emotions with the person who's usually my steadfast emotional sounding board. I could text Alexis about what's going on, but she'd probably just urge me to declare undying passion to Iz instead of listening.

I prop my elbows on the table and drop my head into my hands, giving my forehead a rub before looking at Hope again. "Fuck. Is it bad to say I haven't thought about Iz's birthday at all today?"

She laughs. "Don't sweat the birthday stuff. I've actually got some party plans to go over with you before I leave today. We have pretty much everything prepped, but there are a few last minute tasks to cover."

"Of course, yeah, I want to help with whatever you need."

She smiles. "You're a good friend. I can tell. Iz always goes nuts when you're coming to visit. They get so excited."

My chest tightens at the thought of Iz bouncing around all happy to see me. That's all I want. I just want us to hold onto what we have and face whatever this new stuff is together. I know we can do that. I can feel it the same way I felt Iz's hand in mine last night: shaking, but warm and familiar.

Ready to hold on.

I know I can do that. I know Iz can too. I just need *them* to know it.

I drop my head into my hands again and groan.

Maybe I shouldn't tell Hope so much, but it's not even nine in the morning, I haven't eaten, and my best friend can barely look at me. I need to tell someone *something* or I'm going to end up curled in the fetal position waiting for this weekend to end.

That's not exactly the vibe I want to bring into Iz's birthday party.

"I just wish I knew what they were thinking," I say, shifting to rest my cheek on one of my hands as my shoulders slump even further. "I wish I could have just like, five minutes of x-ray vision into their mind."

Hope laughs again and takes a break from the dishes to sit down across from me. "I think we've all wished for x-ray vision into Iz's mind at one point or another."

I raise an eyebrow. "Oh?"

Hope nods. "I love Iz. Don't get me wrong. I think they're amazing and one of the biggest sweethearts ever, but they just...they make some questionable dating choices, shall we say? I hate feeling like I'm judging them. So do Paulina and Jane, but sometimes the three of us are just here like...Iz, what the hell are you doing?"

She flaps her arms around in exasperation. I laugh at the way the gesture mirrors exactly how I've felt about some of Iz's romantic exploits, even before I realized I might have feelings for them.

"You're right," I agree. "Iz is a total sweetheart, and I think sometimes they end up with people who take advantage of that."

Hope nods. "That's exactly right. I don't know why, but Iz is always ending up with girls who just want to hook up, and meanwhile, Iz is doing their knight in shining armour thing. You know, taking these girls out for picnics and moonlight walks and falling for people who like the attention but not the commitment. It just breaks my heart to see them get hurt again and again, but they always go for the same type of girl."

I've seen it happen over and over, just like Hope has. I've been there on the other end of the phone while Iz cries. I've been the one to tell them it's okay to have feelings. Iz has some of the most beautiful feelings in the world. Their love is pure gold, no matter who they're giving it to, and so many people have thrown that gift away like it's nothing but pebbles.

"Sometimes I think maybe they do it on purpose," I admit.

"Huh?" Hope asks, scooching her chair in closer to the table.

"I just..." I pause and make myself consider what I'm about to say next. This isn't really my story to tell. "Has Iz ever told you about their first girlfriend?"

Hope squints. "Like in high school?"

I nod.

"I think so," she answers. "I think they've mentioned it. It went really badly, right?"

I let out a sharp laugh. "Yeah, that pretty much sums it up."

"Something about prom? Iz got stood up, right?"

I nod. I feel better talking about it now that I know she's already heard the story.

"Prom was the..." I trail off and trace a coffee stain on the table with my finger as I search for the word. "Culmination, shall we say? Iz was crazy about this girl, Sheila, and Sheila strung Iz along for two whole years. I was so pissed at her, but Iz just made excuse after excuse for the way she was acting, and on the one hand, I understood. When you've just come out, an actual queer relationship can feel like this safety net you need to hold onto. Sometimes it's hard to see whether it's even a *good* relationship or not. But I saw it, and it wasn't good. Iz and I fought about it a lot."

I'm staring down at the coffee stain like I'm trying to burn it away with my eyes, and I jump a little when I feel Hope's hand on my arm.

"Sorry. It's just, that must have been hard."

I nod, the memories pulling me back to our shouting matches after school or the times when we'd pass each other in the hall without speaking. It never lasted more than a couple days, but it's the only time we've ever really fought.

I never want to go back to that.

"Finally, towards the end of grade twelve, Iz finally saw the light and told Sheila they needed *something* from her. The two of them hadn't ever even officially been dating. Sheila always had some excuse. I think seeing Iz stand up for themself all of a sudden shocked her, and she ended up asking Iz to prom."

"But it didn't work out," Hope finishes.

I shake my head. "She texted Iz four hours before prom to say she was going with someone else."

"A text?" Hope's mouth drops open. "I didn't know it happened over text."

I grind my teeth together so hard I hear my jaw click as I think back to that day. I was with Iz when their phone pinged with the notification. They were crying so hard I had to pull it out of their hands and read the message myself to figure out what was going on.

"Sheila said things with Iz were 'too much.'" I put it in air quotes. "As if wanting some proof someone's actually into you after two whole years of excuses is too much."

Hope rocks her chair onto its back legs as she slowly shakes her head from side to side. "That is fuuuucked up."

I jerk my chin in a nod. I can feel my blood pressure rising as my temples throb at just the thought of it.

"I can see how that would cause some lasting damage," Hope says, "but I don't see why Iz would keep getting into situations like that now?"

"I don't think Iz *tries* to," I explain, "at least not consciously. I just...I have this theory. I think maybe they date people they know things aren't going to work out with so at least they're not surprised when it fails. I think maybe part of them thinks that's safer than risking it all on someone they might actually have a shot with."

Hope's eyes widen. "Whoa. Are you a psych major?"

I laugh and shake my head. "Political science with a minor in film studies."

She squints at me. "Are you sure you haven't snuck a few psychology courses in there?"

"I think I've just spent a lot of time with Iz."

She crosses her arms over her chest and stares at me, still rocking her chair back and forth in a way that would make my mom shriek about wrecking the furniture. "You guys seem to have a really special friendship. I literally live with Iz, and that theory would never have occurred to me. I thought maybe all we needed to do was get Iz away from the campus sports bar. They're always picking up athletes in there, and college athletes kind of suck at maintaining relationships."

I laugh as I gawk at her. "Aren't you all college athletes?"

She grins. "Yeah, and you should have seen the mess I made of my own love life last semester. I thought if we got Iz away from that scene and hooked them up with some kind of artsy girl or something like that, things would work out great, but what you're saying makes so much sense."

I sigh. "I don't even know how to bring any of this up

without making them mad. It was so awful when we were fighting about Sheila."

"Hey." The front legs of Hope's chair land with a thud on the kitchen floor. "They know you care about them. It might be hard for them to hear, but if you care about them enough to bring it up, I'm sure they'll at least listen."

"And maybe not talk to me again after," I say with a groan.

Hope shrugs. "Maybe, but do you really want to keep all *this* locked up inside you?"

She waves her hand around to indicate a general atmospheric disturbance, and it's pretty spot-on for how I'm feeling. Something about the way she's watching me makes me think she might know 'all this' includes more than just my opinions on who Iz dates.

Instead of panic, I feel weirdly at ease as I offer her a small smile. I really have locked so much up inside me, and this conversation has been like unclenching a pressure valve. It's not enough to take all the worry away, but it helps. I can breathe deeper. I can think clearer.

"Maybe you're right," I say. "It's obviously bothering me so much it's affecting our friendship."

Maybe Iz just needs to know I'm here. Maybe last night wasn't enough. I was ambiguous at best. I was scared of going too far too fast, but maybe I should have been scared of not going far enough.

I'm not one of those girls who will leave Iz behind. I'm not going to make them work for every scrap of reassurance and affection I give out. If they're willing to take this step with me, I'll give them everything I've got.

They deserve that. As terrifying as it will be to say it, they deserve to hear how I feel.

"Do you want some coffee?" Hope's question pulls me

out of my thoughts just in time for us both to hear my stomach growl. She chuckles. "And some breakfast?"

"I'll make myself some toast, if that's okay," I answer. "Oh, and do you guys have tea?"

She tips her head back and raises her eyes to the ceiling. "Do we ever have tea. Jane will love this about you. She's the only non-coffee drinker in the house. She has a whole drawer of that stuff."

She gets up and starts pulling a few drawers open while I slide two slices out of the bag of bread on the counter.

"Aha! It's this one. You'll need to figure this out yourself. I'm not very well-versed in the ways of tea."

I laugh as I walk over to look at all the boxes. "I think I can manage."

"Cool, and before I head to the gym, I'll show you the party stuff we still need help with. I'm just going to go get ready."

I nod. "That would be great. Iz is going to love this party."

She rubs her hands together like she's concocting an evil plan. "They really are. I didn't think we'd actually manage to keep the theme a secret."

"So far so good."

I start getting the toaster set up. Hope heads to the living room but backtracks to the kitchen when I call out her name.

"Yes?" she asks, pushing her glasses up her nose.

"I, uh..." I glance down at the floor. "I just wanted to say thanks for talking with me. I hope I didn't say too much. I wouldn't want to upset Iz, but I just...I think I just really needed to talk to someone."

"Hey, of course." She crosses the few feet of space between us and pulls me into a hug. "Anytime. I know I probably don't seem like the most subtle person, but I promise this is just between us. Iz is one of my best friends too."

She pulls back, and I thank her again.

"Oh, and Marina," she adds just before leaving the room again. "Also just between us, but for what it's worth, I think you and Iz would be great together."

I feel the blood start rising in my cheeks as soon as she says it, and I can't do anything except nod. She heads out, and as I stare down at the bread browning at the toaster, I realize I'm smiling again.

As weird as this morning has been, I'm still smiling, and I can't wait for dinner tonight.

6

Iz

When I woke up next to Marina this morning, I made myself a goal for the day. I looked at her sleeping face on the pillow next to mine, her freckled skin glowing in the red light pouring through my makeshift curtain, and I decided I needed to find a girl to invite to my birthday party.

Marina needs to know I'm not going to get all stupid about this and make a move on her, and the best way to prove that is by making a move on someone else.

It's foolproof, really. I find a date. I tell Marina. Clear lines are established, and we go back to being the kind of friends who can actually look each other in the eye. Last night made it obvious: this friendship means more to us than anything, and we need to protect it.

So I'm going to make sure I do that.

"Hey, Iz!"

I look up from where I've been scrolling through Instagram and spot Olivia Collins, one of the school's star volleyball players, clearing a path through the crowds of people making their way in and of the lobby in the UNS athletics centre.

I've finished up my classes for the day, and I snuck in a quick workout at the gym before I'm due to meet Marina downtown to grab dinner together. I also snuck in a few texts to Olivia during my final chemistry lecture, asking if we could meet up.

One of the perks of dating other athletes is that we're usually in the same places. Adding dates into the mix of practices, games, and schoolwork cramming sessions can be tricky. In some ways, it helps that all the girls I date can often be found in the two buildings I spend as much time in as I do my own house: the athletics centre and our beloved campus sports bar, Mario's.

It does mean I also frequently run into girls I *used* to date, but alas, life always comes with checks and balances.

Olivia Collins falls somewhere in the category of 'girls I used to date.' She's a volleyball goddess with mile-long legs and gorgeous waist-length braids threaded with purple strands that swish back and forth in a hypnotic rhythm as she walks toward me.

I offered to buy her a drink at Mario's a couple months ago, fully expecting her to shoot me down. She's next-level stunning, and I could barely even stammer one of my terrible chemistry pick-up lines to her, but somehow, we ended up going home together.

I thought maybe we'd end up as more than hook-up buddies. We got to the point where we were seeing movies together and going for workouts at the gym, but then she got busy with training and started cancelling more and more often. It never officially ended, and I wish I didn't feel the sting of rejection looking at her now, but I do. That's always the worst part when things turn out like this:

telling myself I don't care and then realizing I've still managed to get hurt.

I ball one of my hands into a fist in the sleeve of my jacket, squeezing hard until the pain fades away.

This is an emergency, and I know Olivia hardly ever says no to a party. She'll probably show up with half the volleyball team, and it'll be a fun birthday where I laugh and dance and flirt with a girl while hanging out with all my friends.

The usual. No chance of me being an *idiota* with Marina—or as we like to say, a dumby dumb dumb.

"God, I haven't seen you in so long." Olivia reaches the spot where I'm leaning against the wall and pulls me into a hug. "How are you doing?"

"I'm, uh, good." I try to hide how surprised I am by the hug and end up giving her a dorky pat on the back before she pulls away. "How are you?"

"I'm great. Training is as crazy as ever. You're lucky lacrosse is all done by the end of the first semester."

"Yeah, not gonna lie. I miss playing so much already, but it kind of takes over your life."

She nods. "For sure."

But I still made time for you.

I don't want to go down that train of thought, but it swoops into the station of my brain anyway. I was just as busy as Olivia, but I made the time.

Because I cared.

I always care. I always care, and that's the problem. I ask for too much. *I'm* too much.

Olivia is telling me about some big party the boys' hockey team hosted last weekend, and as I try to focus on the words she's saying, it really hits me: what strangers we are.

Just a couple months ago, we were joking around side

by side on the treadmills and kissing in between dumbbell sets. I was imagining what it would be like to have her as my girlfriend, and now we're nothing at all. Maybe we were never really anything to begin with.

I never want to look at Marina the way I'm looking at Olivia now: like she's someone I used to know.

"Yeah, you're right," I answer, tuning back into Olivia's story just in time to catch her comment about me missing the party. "I'll have to make all my housemates go to the next one. By the way, speaking of parties, what are you up to tomorrow night?"

She crosses her arms over her chest and leans against the wall beside me, lifting one of her perfect eyebrows. "Do you have an invitation for me, Iz?"

"I, um..." I clear my throat. "Well, my housemates are throwing me this birthday party tomorrow night, and it's pretty much an open invitation for anyone who wants to come, so I thought maybe you'd like to stop by. You can bring whoever you want from the team too."

She nods a couple times and then smiles. "I'd like that. To be honest, I've been missing you, Iz. I was happy you texted today. We had some good times last semester."

It's stupid to feel a flutter in my chest. It's stupid to stand here grinning at her like an excited teenager, but I still do. It's not even about *her*; it's the microsecond of hope that maybe I didn't read this all wrong. Again. Maybe she really was into me. Maybe I didn't fuck it up.

Maybe things weren't the same as they were with Sheila in high school, or everyone else since.

"Well, I'm happy you answered my text."

She tips her head back and laughs. "You're cute, Iz. I'll try to stop by the party. What street are you guys on again?"

I give her the address, and she wishes me happy

birthday before heading for the locker room. I stay standing where I am, watching the rushing crowds of students for a few seconds after she's gone. Then I roll my shoulders back and make my way out of the building.

Step one complete. Now for part two: tell Marina.

I pull my phone out as I walk up the stone path between two snow-coated lawns. In the spring and summer, the campus lawns are always covered with students playing Frisbee and having picnics, but in the depths of February, everyone sticks to the paths and huddles in their coats. I pull one of my gloves off so I can send a text to Marina and let her know I'm on my way.

She sends a reply to say 'See you soon!' a couple seconds later followed by a GIF of a puppy waiting in a window. She's a big fan of GIFs. I laugh to myself as I stick my phone back in my pocket, some of the tension in my shoulders relaxing.

Marina and I are going to be okay, just like we said last night. We don't get many visits during the school year, and now we can put all this weirdness behind us and going back to enjoying these few days we're lucky enough to have together.

The walk to my favourite sushi place in Halifax only takes about fifteen minutes. It would be even faster if there weren't so many damn hills in this city. Traversing the downtown core is like navigating a mountain climbing expedition, but the reward is the waterfront at the very bottom. It's not all that exciting in the winter, but in summer, nothing beats living near the ocean.

"Hey girl heyyyy!" I call out when I step inside the restaurant and spot Marina in a booth by the window.

The place is a mix between modern and cozy, with bright white walls draped with fake vines and mismatched pillows on all the seats. Every booth has a weird, trendy basket light thing hanging down from the ceiling above it, and the rainbow-coloured wooden chopsticks they give out make my gay heart happy.

"Oh my God, Iz, when are you going to stop saying hey girl hey?"

"What?" I joke as settle myself into the booth. "You don't like it?"

"You just pronounce it really weirdly," she teases me.

I shrug. "I have no idea what you're talking about."

She laughs and continues flipping through the menu she has open on the table. "It is pretty cute."

I make myself take a few a slow, even breaths even as my heart starts to pound.

Friends call each other cute. It's no big deal. I don't have to be weird about it.

"Do you know what you're getting already?" I ask.

"If it's okay with you, I thought we could do a platter together, and maybe split some appetizers?"

"That would be great." I leave my menu untouched in front of me. "I love everything they make here, so I'm down for whatever."

Marina raises an eyebrow. "I'll be nice and try not to take that as a challenge to find something you won't eat."

I put a hand on my chest and fake being overcome with gratitude. "Wow. Thank you for your generosity."

"You are most welcome."

We both crack up as she goes back to looking at the menu. I shrug my coat off and lean back against the vinyl seat, letting some more of the tension slip away. I'm having dinner with my favourite person in the world. I should chill the fuck out and enjoy it.

"So how was your day?" I ask.

"Uneventful. I worked on some papers and maaaaybe some party stuff, but I'm not telling you about that."

"Marinaaaa!" I brace my hands on the table and rock back and forward. "*Por Dios!* You guys are driving me crazy with this party theme! I need to know!"

She wags her finger at me. "Soon enough. Soon enough."

I just groan in response.

"What about your day?" she asks once I'm done with the drama. "How did your classes go?"

"They were good. Chem was as complicated as ever, but I enjoyed it. I, uh..." I trace one of my fingertips over the restaurant's name on the front of the menu. "I actually have some news."

She grins. "Well, what do you know? I have some news too."

"Oh? Well you can go first."

I can feel myself starting to sweat. It's not like I haven't told Marina about girls I've asked out before; it's rare I *don't* tell her, but something about this is turning my hands into clammy little blobs I have to wipe on my jeans under the table.

I could be imagining it, but Marina looks nervous about her news too—nervous, and maybe excited. Her eyes have gone all bright, and she's leaning in closer over the table.

She looks kissable, and that's exactly why I have to tell her I invited a girl to my party. I have to stop noticing her like this.

"Nuh-uh." She shakes her head. "You mentioned yours first, so you have to go first."

"Lucky me."

She laughs, and it sounds like music. "Go on, Iz. Out with it."

My heart starts pounding so loud I can't hear the electro-pop music pumping through the speakers anymore. I can feel my throat getting thick, like it's swelling up in protest of what I'm about to say.

Which doesn't make any sense. This is *good* news. Marina and I both want things to be normal, and for years, it's been normal for me to talk to her about my dating life.

"Iz?"

I look up at the sound of my name and realize I've been glaring down at the menu like I'm decoding the secrets of the universe. Marina is watching me with her head tilted to the side and her eyebrows drawn together.

"Is everything okay?"

"Oh. Yeah." I roll my shoulders back a couple times. "I just zoned out there. Sorry about that. So, uh, yeah, you remember that girl Olivia I was kind of seeing for a bit?"

I expect her to roll her eyes and come up with some sassy comment about Olivia being so flaky. Marina has always been good at getting me to laugh at my own catastrophes.

Neither of us is laughing now. Instead of making a joke like I expect her to, she just nods and presses her lips together. I don't know if it's the lighting in here, but I swear her face gets a shade paler.

I roll my shoulders again. "Well, I asked her to come to the party, and she said yes. It's not like an actual date or anything, but yeah, she'll be there."

The door hasn't moved, but I feel like a surge of icy air right off the frigid ocean has swept into the room. Marina's lips are pressed so tight together they're going white.

I'm fucking up.

I can feel it like the words are engraved on an iron sign hanging around my neck, spelt out for everyone to see, but I don't know *what* I'm fucking up. This should have made things better.

"I didn't think I missed her, to be honest," I add,

figuring maybe I need to make things more clear. Every word feels like it's echoing in the chilly silence between us. "But it was nice to see her today."

"It was *nice*?"

Marina's voice is just a whisper, but it still makes me jump. Her pale cheeks have started flooding with colour, but her eyes are even colder now. She narrows them as she stares at me.

"Really, Iz? It was *nice*?"

"I..." I trail off when I realize I have no idea what to say. I have no idea what she *wants* me to say.

She shakes her chin from side to side, so subtly I almost don't see it.

"I can't believe you went back to her," she mutters.

Something in me sparks and spits in protest at that.

"I didn't *go back to her*." There's no change in Marina's expression when I speak. It's almost like she's looking straight through me now. "I asked her to come to a party, and it was nice. I'm not declaring my love to her, okay? I'm not stupid."

She just keeps staring at me, and I feel my own face start to heat up.

"I just thought it would be fun to have her at the party. I learned my lesson with her. I'm not expecting any more than that."

"Oh, I'm sure you'll have *fun*, Iz."

I blink at the venom in her voice. I've never heard her sound so sharp before. She's still barely speaking above a whisper, but I feel every word like a barb in my skin.

"What's that supposed to mean?"

"It means that nothing's changed, and I..." She stumbles over the end of her sentence, and I see a flash of pain cross her face.

My hand twitches where I'm gripping my knees under

the table. I want to reach for her. It happens on instinct: when she's hurt, I'm there. When I'm hurt, she's there. It's how we've always been together. I feel her pain like it's my own.

"I thought it had changed," she mumbles.

"M-Marina." I take a shaky breath to stop myself from stammering. "You thought what changed?"

We're on a tight rope again, caught somewhere between safety and disaster, tipping toward a freefall with every word.

"I..."

Her eyes are so big. They could swallow me up. I could fall right into them, and there'd be no going back.

"Never mind." She glances away, shaking her head.

"Marina—"

"I said *never mind, Iz*." I jump again when she snaps at me. I've never heard her snap like that before.

"I—"

"Whatever," she interrupts. "Bring her to the party. It's your birthday. Do what you want. Have a nice time."

Our food shows up just then, and as the waiter settles the plates on the table in front of us, I watch Marina avoid my eyes. I've never felt so far away from her.

"This looks good," she says, her gaze pinned to a plate of sushi as the waiter heads back to the kitchen. Her voice is flat, and it doesn't give me anything to go on.

I'm spinning out with nothing to stop me.

My appetite is long gone, but I pluck some pieces up with my chopsticks and drop them on my plate just to have something to do. Marina does the same, the silence stretching on between us. I chew and chew on my first piece, but my throat won't let me swallow. I can't taste the rice in my mouth.

"I'm not actually that hungry anymore," Marina says after getting through a few pieces.

I shake my head and finish sipping the water I've grabbed. "Me neither."

"We could get it to go?"

All the sting is gone from her tone, leaving an emptiness instead. I can't tell which is worse.

"Sure."

I nod and look around for the waiter. After I've asked for a to-go box and assured him there's nothing wrong with the food, I turn back to Marina.

"I forgot you said you had news too. What's up?"

That might get us back on track. We've fallen into a conversational chasm, and I need something to pull us back out.

"Oh. Yeah." She stares down at a bowl of edamame, nudging the beans around with her chopsticks without eating any. "I, uh, forget what I was gonna say."

7

Marina

"Okay, Marina, your turn!"

Jane motions for me to step up to where she's holding out a blindfold. There's a rudimentary, life-size drawing of Iz done in Sharpies tacked to the living room wall behind her. The drawing is covered in stuck-on cut-outs in the shape of Iz's favourite pair of Jordans.

'Pin the Jordans on Iz' is just one feature of the Jordans-themed birthday party that's now in full swing. The red Solo cups in everyone's hands have little Jordans stickers on the side, and there's a sneaker-shaped piñata hanging from the ceiling, waiting to be destroyed.

A pop playlist is blasting so loud I can barely hear Jane calling to me, and the living room is packed with UNS students crowded in shoulder to shoulder. The place smells like a college party: that signature tang of spilt beer and sweat mixed with the heady, smoky overtone of what my mom calls 'the devil's cabbage.'

I cough as I step close enough for Jane to tie the strip of fabric around my eyes and press a cut-out into my hands.

"You ready to spin?" she asks, leaning in close so I can hear her. Her breath tickles my ear.

With the scratchy blindfold cutting off my vision, all my other senses go into overdrive. The music is now so loud I can feel the bass reverberating in my skull, and the smell of someone's beer-filled Solo cup makes my stomach churn as they pass by. My white skinny jeans and lacy black shirt feel stuffy and tight in the stifling room.

I want to pull the fabric off my eyes and run out of here, but Jane is already gripping my shoulders to twirl me around. I stumble over my feet as she settles me in the right direction. I inch forward, one hand braced in front of me until my palm thumps against the wall.

I'm sweating now. I can't hear anything except the music and the low roar of voices, but my brain is trying to convince me I can make out the sound of laughter nearby. It's just like when I'd swear I could hear people laughing in the hallways back in high school. Over and over again, Iz would tell me no one was making fun of me, but I'd still find a way to make it real to myself.

Just like I'm doing now. It hasn't been this bad in a long time, but as I slide my hand along the wall, searching for the right spot to stick the shoe, I'm sure the whole room is laughing at the stupid fat girl.

Stupid. Stupid. Stupid.

That's all I've been able to think since that disastrous excuse for a dinner with Iz last night. I thought we'd talk about our feelings for each other. I thought we already *had*. I thought our conversation in Iz's bed would flow into dinner yesterday and end with us walking out of the restaurant holding hands.

I seriously thought we might have our first real kiss yesterday. I knew we'd have a lot to figure out, but I thought we were doing it. I thought something had changed.

Then Iz mentioned inviting that girl to the party, and it hit me: how stupid I'd been. Nothing is different. Iz is still chasing some girl who doesn't give a shit about them, and I'm still the best friend who's there to pick up the pieces.

Every. Damn. Time.

That's what we are. That's how it's always been, and I was dumb enough to think it could change overnight. I was dumb enough to think it could change at all. Iz and I have had *moments* even before the New Year's kiss, and it never made anything different. I don't know why I let myself get so caught up in thinking this time would.

For lack of a better term, I was a dumby dumb dumb.

A raging, tangled mass of emotions I can't separate from one another roars to life inside me like an overheating engine, and I smack the cut-out against the wall, beyond caring about getting it in the right spot.

I hear Jane whooping, and when I peel off the blind-fold, I see I've put the shoe exactly in line with the wonky outline of Iz's foot. No one else has gotten that close.

A sharp laugh bursts out of me as I take in the sight. I know Iz. Even with my eyes shut, I know them better than anyone else.

Which means I should have seen this coming.

"Congratulations!" Jane takes the blindfold and hands me a mini, single-serving size bottle of Smirnoff. "Anyone who gets it on a foot wins one of these!"

"Oh, thanks." I clutch the bottle in my hand and shuffle out of the way as she gets the next person set up.

I find a spot where I'm at minimal risk for getting whacked with anyone's elbows or having a beer acciden-tally dumped on my shirt. I pick at the lacy black hem of my top and tuck the vodka into my pocket before using my other hand to fan myself. I was proud of this outfit when I put it on. It's the perfect mix of classy and fun—just the kind of thing I imagine Miss Audrey Hepburn would approve of if she were picking out a modern wardrobe.

No one else is dressed like this. At least ninety percent of the people here are UNS athletes, and most of them are wearing UNS tops paired with jeans or sweatpants. My clothes make it extra clear I'm not one of these people. I'm not even shaped like these people. Jane is considered a 'curvy' athlete, but even she's barely plus-sized.

I keep tugging on my shirt as I scan the room. I saw Hope not too long ago, and I stand on my tiptoes to see if I can spot her again. I don't really feel like talking to anyone, but I could at least stand there and nod along with her and whoever she's hanging out with.

I can't see the teal tips of her hair anywhere in the crowd. I'm right next to the entryway, and when the front door opens to let another half-dozen people surge into the packed house, a blast of cold air hits my skin and makes my body sing out in relief. I take what feels like my first deep breath all day and close my eyes for just a second.

I can do this.

I can get through this party. I already got through the silent awkwardness of the rest of the night with Iz yesterday. We came home, studied on our own for a few hours, and then went to bed without exchanging more than five complete sentences.

Today wasn't much better. I was supposed to keep Iz busy for a few hours while the party got set up, but I managed to get Jane to take them out instead by insisting I felt like I hadn't done my fair share of party prep.

I straight up avoided time with my best friend on their birthday. I still have a framed cross-stitch of the two of us sitting wrapped at the bottom of my suitcase because I couldn't find the right moment to give it to them.

Maybe there won't be a right moment. Maybe we won't bounce back from this. Maybe we've wedged something between us like a splinter that only gets deeper the more you try to pull it out.

Maybe we'll just need to live with that thorn stuck under our skin forever.

My stomach lurches, and I brace a hand on the wall behind me to steady my shaky knees.

I need to get out of here.

The whole crowd is going crazy over an Ariana Grande song, but I barely hear the chorus as I weave my way through the jumping and swaying bodies to get to the door. I pass right by the foot of the staircase and glance up at the people milling on the steps, waving Solo cups in the air and dancing along to the music. I spot Paulina with some jock guy's hands on her hips, and then I make the mistake of looking to the very top of the stairs.

Iz is grinning like a king surveying their kingdom, Solo cup in hand and the absolute Pinterest fail of a papier-mâché Jordans-themed crown Paulina made perched on their head.

They're wearing a blue short-sleeved button-down patterned with little frogs. I got them that shirt a few years ago, and I feel my face crumple as I think back to the look on their face when they pulled it out of the bag.

You know me so well.

That's what they said, and in that moment, it felt like we knew all each other's secrets, like there was no need to hide and never would be. We'd be that safe place where everything always made sense.

I keep watching them at the top of the stairs, my eyes

stinging in warning as they turn their head to speak to someone and I notice the girl beside them for the first time.

Olivia Collins.

I didn't need Iz to point her out when she walked in the room. I just knew. She's gorgeous: tall, thin, and athletic. Most of the girls Iz dates are athletic.

Most of them don't look anything like me.

I keep staring like I'm watching a car crash unfold as Iz slings an arm around Olivia's shoulders and lifts their cup to start shouting along with the song. They turn their head to look down the staircase again, and I don't have time to move away before their eyes lock on mine.

Their face freezes in place, Ariana Grande's lyrics left unspoken as they watch me. Olivia is still swaying along beside them, but they've gone completely still. Everything has gone still.

They could clear a path down those steps and come meet me. They could leave it all behind. We could move forward together.

But they don't.

They don't, and they aren't going to.

I make the mistake of blinking, and the hot tears clinging to my eyes slide down my cheeks. The room blurs as I turn away and head to the entryway closet. It's full to bursting, coats packed inside in a jumbled heap. There are coats scattered all over the floor too. I dig through the closet, swearing under my breath. I'm sure I look like a crazy person, but there's no one here to care. I find my coat buried at the very back of the closet and don't bother pulling it on before I yank the door open and step into the frigid night.

It's almost as loud in the tiny front yard as it is in the house, but the noise has a dull quality to it, all the edges smoothed until it's nothing but a thumping, shapeless distraction. The cold air raises the hairs on my bare arms and makes my lungs burn as I stand in the glow of the pink string lights in the front window, gulping down uneven gasps of air.

I can already feel the snow seeping into the thin sneakers I was wearing in the house as I stand hunched against the wall. The tears streaming out of my eyes burn my cold cheeks and then turn icy as they lose their heat on their way down my face. My nose is running like a faucet, but I just let it all happen, waiting for the worst to pass.

Stupid. Stupid. Stupid.

I haven't felt this bad about myself in a long time. I didn't know I *could* still feel this bad about myself.

The music is practically shaking the wall I'm leaning on. I have to get out of here. I don't know how I'm supposed to go back in there and sleep in that house with them tonight, but I'll figure it out later. I slip my arms into my coat and head up the short path to the sidewalk. I've just started down the street, picking my way around clumps of ice, when the sound of the door opening makes me pause.

"Marina!" a voice shouts above the temporary increase in volume before the door shuts again and the night returns to relative quiet. "Wait!"

It's the wrong voice.

I look over my shoulder and find Hope shimmying into her coat as she jogs over to join me.

"What's up? I saw you leaving, and I just thought I..."

She trails off as she takes in the sight of what I'm sure is my very tear and snot-streaked face. There's probably some mascara mixed in there too.

"I'm fine," I say, which is so obviously far from the truth I'm surprised Hope doesn't laugh like I'm making a joke. "Just, uh, needed some air. I'm going for a walk."

"Uh-huh." She tilts her head to the side and looks me up and down before she finishes zipping up her coat. "You mind if I walk with you? I could use some air too. It's so hot in there."

I nod, and we fall into step beside each other. I let Hope take the lead in navigating since she's the one who lives here.

"So, the party is kind of a flop, huh?" she says as we pass under the yellow-orange glow of a streetlight.

"A flop?" My breath forms a cloud in the air in front of me. "It's packed in there."

"Yeah, *too* packed." She lets out a frustrated sigh. "I don't even know half those people, and neither does Iz. Most of them don't even know it's a birthday party. I'm all for a rager now and then, but I think we were all planning on something more personal. We haven't even been able to bring the cake out yet."

I chuckle at the thought of the cake Hope finished up while Jane took Iz out today. The chocolate interior seemed to be fine, but the icing was a bit of a disaster. The Jordans Hope drew on top look like they were salvaged from a fire, or possibly a trash compactor.

"At least Iz is having fun," I say, all my amusement fading as I think back to them dancing with Olivia at the top of the stairs.

My eyes start stinging again, but I force the tears back this time.

"You think Iz is having fun?" Hope's forehead creases as she glances at me.

"I mean...yes? They looked pretty damn happy last time I saw them."

"Huh. When I talked to them half an hour ago, they said they were sick of the crowd. I said we could break up the party, but they didn't want to be rude." She shrugs. "I don't think it's rude to end your own birthday party. It's Iz's party, after all."

"Huh."

I stay quiet as we round a corner onto a new street. Our crunching footsteps are the only sounds besides the distant rumble of cars downtown. The street is lined with old-fashioned row houses and a few newer models, but they all have a 'here there be students' vibe to them: UNS Lobsters flags in the windows, crates of beer bottles out with the recycling, and dilapidated, snow-dusted couches dotting a few front lawns.

"You don't have to answer this," Hope says as we leave the pool of light under a streetlamp, "but I take it things aren't stellar between you and Iz right now?"

"Um..." I consider deflecting the question, but I don't have enough energy left to do anything except tell the truth. "No. No, they're not."

"Did you have a fight?"

I test a suspicious-looking patch of snow with one of my shoes, and sure enough, there's a slippery layer of pure ice underneath. I lead the way around the hazard.

"Kind of?" I answer. "To be honest, I don't know what to call it. It was just bad."

She chuckles. "Yeah, I get that."

"Last night at dinner, I wanted to talk about...us, but they...they went straight to telling me they asked that Olivia girl to come to the party."

"Wait, what? Iz asked Olivia to come?" Hope's eyes go wide. "Like as their date?"

"They said it wasn't as an official date, but they just..." I suck in a breath, wincing at the pain the memory brings up. "They were talking about it like it was supposed to make me happy, or like, impressed or something? It was so weird. It was like some weird...*offering*, and I don't know what the hell they meant by it. To my understanding, we had already kind of admitted that we...that there's...we feel..."

Hope nudges my shoulder with hers to cut off my stammering. "I know. You don't have to spell it out for me if it's too hard."

"Thanks." I nod, letting the chilly air cool the warmth rising in my cheeks. "So yeah, that's where I thought we were, but then they went and pulled this thing with Olivia, and now I don't know what the hell is going on. Maybe I was totally wrong about it all."

I keep trudging up the snowy sidewalk, my heart thumping against my chest under my coat. I can't stop the avalanche of thoughts from escaping now that I've started. It doesn't matter that I don't know Hope very well. It doesn't matter that I'm talking so fast all my sentences are starting to get jumbled together. I just need to get this out.

"Maybe I ruined everything for no good reason. Maybe I need to accept that all we're ever going to be is friends and keep the rest to myself. I've done it for so long now. Maybe I just have to keep doing it."

"Marina."

I only realize Hope has stopped walking when I look around at the sound of my name and find her standing a few feet behind me.

"Marina," she repeats, "it's not in your head, okay? I can promise you that. Anyone who's seen you and Iz together can tell you that."

"Except Iz."

She closes the distance between us and lifts one side of her mouth in a half-smile, but her eyes are filled with a sympathy so sincere it's hard to look at. "Yeah, apparently anyone except Iz, but that's not your fault."

"I just..." I look down at my soaked sneakers. I don't

have much longer before my feet will be totally numb. "I don't think I can keep doing this, and it scares me. I don't think I can keep being there for them while I feel like this. When I think about having to let this go and watch them...I just can't keep doing that."

"You don't have to, you know." Hope's voice is quieter now. "You don't have to do that. You're allowed to say it's not working for you."

I take a deep breath. I didn't realize I'd been waiting to hear that from someone before I could consider it myself. "But if I tell Iz that, and they can't accept it, then..."

"Then that's on Iz." Hope spreads her hands. "Look, I love Iz, but to be honest, I think they're really dropping the ball here."

I huff a laugh. "Was that supposed to be a lacrosse joke?"

Hope grins. "No, but now that you mention it, it totally works. You and Iz are best friends. You're a team, and a team is supposed to play together, even when the game gets tough."

We blink at each other for a second before we both double over laughing.

"Oh my god," Hope wheezes. "That's the cheesiest thing I've ever said."

"It was like you used some kind of generic sports speech generator," I joke, which sends us into another laughing fit.

"Wow." Hope straightens up after a moment and swipes at her eyes. "My bad. That was awful, but I do mean it. You're allowed to draw a line, and who knows? Maybe that's what Iz needs to help them step up."

"You mean that's what they need to get their head in the game?" I tease.

"Yeah, exactly." She laughs again as she starts leading

the way up the street. "Maybe that's what they need to stop dropping that damn ball."

We turn another corner, and I realize we've done a lap around the block. I can hear the music from the party again, and the pink glow emitting from the Babe Cave's front window is like a homing beacon.

"Why the hell didn't I put my boots on?" I grumble as I urge my frozen feet to hold out for a few more metres.

"It's a nasty night," Hope says. "You should stand by the heater when you get inside. Maybe do a few shots of whiskey."

I shiver. "Normally I'm not the type, but I might take you up on that."

We reach the tiny excuse for a front yard, and Hope's about to bound up the steps to the door when it swings open. A solid wall of noise greets us, and it takes me a second to recognize the person calling something over their shoulder back into the house.

"Oh." Iz blinks when they turn around and spot Hope and I stopped in our tracks, standing there like oversized lawn ornaments. "Hey."

I can't do anything except nod.

They step out of the doorframe, and that's when I notice they're wearing boots and a coat. Hope moves over to make room for them to come down the stairs.

"Hey, birthday person," she says, not-so-subtly glancing between the two of us. "What are you doing out here?"

Iz also keeps glancing at me. "Just needed a little air."

"Well, hopefully you wanted cold air. It's nasty out here. In fact, I was just going to get some fortifying beverages prepared for Marina and me. Would you like one?"

"Hmm." Iz rocks back and forth on their heels. "I'm think I'm good, but uh, could I talk to you, Marina?"

I try not to gulp. Nothing good ever followed the phrase 'Can I talk to you?'

I nod again. A moment of silence passes before Hope clears her throat.

"Come find me when you want your whiskey, Marina."

"Will do," I call without taking my eyes off Iz. I can't seem to do anything except look at Iz. "Thanks."

She heads back inside, and then it's just the two of us alone in the yard.

8

Iz

Marina's face is catching some of the pink glow from the lights in the living room window, and her cheeks are flushed from the cold. Her eyes are shining, and I don't know if the glimmer is a reflection or tears or something I don't have a name for. All I know is that in this moment, I miss her more than I've ever missed anyone before.

It's only been a few days of crossed wires, but I feel like the half the country has come between us again. She's here and she's not here. We're us and we're not us.

I don't know how to be me without her.

The thought reverberates in my head, and maybe the echo effect is just a result of the beers I've had tonight, but it's true. We're wrapped up in each other, like two trees planted side by side in a park. As we got older, our branches twisted together, and so did our roots. I feel hurt when she's hurt. I grow when she grows.

"You wanted to talk?"

Even with the noise of the party raging on behind us, her voice is a shock in the otherwise quiet street.

"I...yeah."

I don't even know what I want to talk about. I just know I never want to see her looking at me the way she did from the bottom of the stairs back in the house. By the time I got down there, she was already gone. I ran into the yard in just my socks, but I couldn't see her. My phone has been missing for the past two hours, so I couldn't even send a text.

I waited by the door, but she never came back in. I was heading out here on my way to look for her, my head spinning with a thousand apologies. Now none of them seem like enough. I don't even know what she wants. I don't know where we're supposed to go from here, and the longer we go without talking about it, the further she gets from me. I almost expect her to start fading away like a chemistry experiment gone wrong. All it takes is one mistake, and you're left with nothing but vapour.

I clear my throat. "Are you...okay?"

She watches me for a moment, then another moment, and then she shakes her head. "I'm not."

"I'm sorry." I glance down at the trodden-down snow under my feet. "I know the party has gotten out of control. It's not what I wanted either, and I'm sorry we haven't gotten much time together. That was rude of me. I want to hang out with you for the rest of the—"

"It's not about the party, Iz." She sighs. "Not really. It's about...you and me."

A wailing siren starts going off in my head, screaming out a warning. We're getting closer and closer to a fire now, and it's going to burn us up. I know it. We haven't even talked about this yet, and we're already singed. We're already crumbling. This can't be how we fix it.

I know how it goes when I become a 'you and me' with people. I know where I end up.

"You mean about...dinner?" I ask, my voice climbing up an octave. "I know it was awkward. I'm sorry. You're probably sick of hearing about girls from me. I know I vent to you a lot, probably too much. I can stop. I—"

"Goddammit, Iz!"

Her shout cuts off my frantic rambling. My words are just a distraction, a verbal floodgate to stop what's coming next, and it doesn't seem to be working.

I know what she's going to say. Maybe I've always known. Maybe part of me wants to say it too, but there are no take-backs here. There's no trial run. She's not some girl who's going to fade into the background of my life once we've played this out.

She's Marina.

I need her.

"Listen to me, Iz." She steps close enough that our faces are only a few inches apart. Even in the semi-darkness, I can see the freckles dusting her nose. "I can't keep going on like this. I can't keep waiting. I can't keep hoping. I can't keep thinking we're taking one step forward when really we're taking five steps back. It's exhausting."

I blink. "You think I'm...exhausting?"

A flash of tenderness softens the hard set of her features for a second. "No, Iz, not you, but this"—she gestures between us—"this is. This hurts, and I have to draw a line somewhere. I see that now. I'm just hurting both of us when I play along."

She steps away from me and spreads her hands, tipping her head back as she closes her eyes. She stands there breathing for a few seconds, and I start to wonder if I'm supposed to say something. I've just opened my mouth when she looks at me again, and all my words fail me when I see the mix of pain, hope, longing, and *love* in the way she's watching me now.

I can't breathe. The cold night air settles in my lungs, refusing to move.

No one has ever looked at me like that.

"I can't play along with this game where we get closer and closer to what we could be, what we're *meant* to be, and then you back away. I can't keep reaching my hand out and not having you catch it. I want to give the whole fucking world, Iz, and you know what? I think you could give it to me too. I *know* you could, even if you don't believe it. I know you're scared, and I know you've been hurt so many times. I know that, all right? I've been there for all of it, but now I need you to be there for me. I need you to be there for us."

Shut this down. Shut this down. Shut this down.

It's the only thing I can think. Her words have me even more breathless than before, but I need to speak. I need to stop this. If we go any further, we won't be able to go back.

If we go any further, we could lose everything.

"I'm—I'm sorry," I stammer. "I know I've probably monopolized our friendship sometimes. I want to be there for you, Marina. That's so important to me. I—"

"Iz, that is *not* what I'm talking about, and you know it." Her voice has gone from determined to desperate. Her hands flutter at her sides like she's trying to pull words out of the air. "Please stop pretending you don't. I don't care what else happens. I just need to know I'm not alone here. I feel crazy, Iz, fucking *crazy*, and I hate it."

"Marina, I—"

"No, just *listen*, okay?" she begs. "Just listen. Iz...this isn't how I wanted to say this, but I don't think I have a choice. I...I...Sometimes, I just stop and...and *stare* at you. I can't help it. I look at you, and my whole fucking life falls into place. I'm not saying it doesn't scare me, but it's real and it's true, and it's also the best fucking thing I've ever felt. I want to be with you, Iz—not just as your friend. I want us to be more, and I'm tired of dancing around that. I'm tired of trying to read into every moment. That's not us. We're supposed to be honest with each other. We're supposed to trust each other. You're my best friend, and I love you, but I'm also...I think I'm in love with you, Iz."

I stumble backwards, my ankles colliding with the edge of the bottom step and almost sending me sprawling in the snow. I catch my balance just in time, but I still feel like I'm falling. The ground is dropping out from under me, opening up into a bottomless chasm, and I just fall and fall and fall.

I fall through every moment that brought us here: playing on blankets with dump trucks and dolls, walking into the first day of middle school side by side, every pool party and sleepover, every high school drama and night spent staying up way too late talking about the rest of our lives.

Every dream and promise. Every friendship bracelet and Valentine. Every moment her fingers have twined with mine and we've taken on the world hand in hand. Even the arguments and the tears and those awful days when we didn't speak are part of our story.

Our story.

The story of us.

When she hurts, I hurt. When she grows, I grow.

It's love. There's always been love between us.

"Marina..." I can't do more than whisper her name.

"I needed you to know." She's whispering too, and there's a stillness to her, like a moment of peace after a storm. "I can't hide it anymore. I don't want to."

She's building a bridge for me, and all I have to do is cross it, but I stay stuck where I am.

Love doesn't go well for me. It never has. I don't work

as an *us*, and she needs to know it. She needs to know why I've been taking a step back for every step forward.

"We...we're friends."

I know I should elaborate. I know she deserves more, but that's all that comes out.

"I know, Iz. I'm saying I want to be more than that."

"But you...I..." My throat has gone so dry I have to pause and force myself to swallow. "You've seen me try to date people, Marina. You know what happens. There's something *wrong* with me. I'm too much, or maybe I'm not enough, or—or something, but it just doesn't work. Why would you want that?"

She still has that calm, distant look to her, like she's gone somewhere beyond me, and I can't find what it takes to follow her. She's vapour in my hands.

"There is nothing wrong with you, Iz. You have *so* much love in you. I know you do. I think you're just scared to let it out."

I gawk at her. "But I've tried. So many times. You've seen me try."

She shakes her head. "I think you only give that love to people you know can't handle it."

That pricks like a pin in my skin, and I can hear the tension in my voice when I speak. The flicker of doubt in Marina's eyes tells me she hears it too.

"That's what you think I'm doing? You think I'm doing it on purpose?" I murmur, shaking my head. "You've seen how broken this has made me, and you think I'm stupid enough to keep doing in on purpose?"

"Iz, that's not what I meant. You're not stupid. You just—"

"I thought you said there was nothing wrong with me," I interrupt.

I'm being an asshole. I know I am, but I can't stop. It's

easier to fight with her than it is to process those words she said that shifted everything.

I think I'm in love with you, Iz.

She realigned my whole world in one sentence. She turned my axis upside down, and I don't even know how to stand anymore. I don't know to breathe or think or be. Everything is rearranging. My head is a city on fire, sending everything I know scattering out into a new world.

"I think you got hurt, Iz. That's what I think." She's done whispering now. I can hear the fire in her voice too. "I think you're still hurting, and now you're hurting me too. Neither of us deserves that."

She's right.

I recognize the truth, but I don't know what to do with it. I don't know what to do with any of this.

One voice speaking the truth isn't enough to drown out voice after voice telling me I'm too much, I'm not normal, I'm not wanted. That's what happens when I love. I heard it from Sheila years ago, and everything since has just proved she was right.

"I'm scared, Marina."

She nods. "I know."

"I'm so scared. I'm—I'm too scared. I don't...I can't...I just *can't*." I'm begging, pleading for her to understand why this will never work.

If we do this, we'll lose it all.

I see her fingers twitch like she wants to reach for me, but then she clenches her hands into a fist and pulls it into the sleeve of her coat.

"Okay, then. You can't, but that means I can't do this."

I don't have time to ask her what *this* is. I try to speak as she moves past me up the stairs, but part of me already knows.

This is us: everything we are and have been.

And she can't do it anymore.

9

Marina

"Oh damn. You really look like you could use this whiskey."

I glance up from hunching over my suitcase in Iz's room and see Hope standing in the doorway. She's got a Solo cup in each hand.

A manic laugh bursts out of me, and Hope's eyes widen. I clear my throat and straighten up, doing my best not to keep looking like insane.

"You'd be right about that. I would love some whiskey."

"It's Jack and Coke." She hands me one of the cups and clinks her to mine. "Bottoms up!"

I'm not much of a drinker, but I tip the cup back and down the whole thing in a few sips. The sweetness of the Coke gives way to the burning sensation of the whiskey travelling down my throat.

"So, uh, what's up with the suitcase?" Hope nods at my stuff after eyeing my empty cup. She's still got more than half her drink left.

I follow her gaze to my open suitcase lying behind me

on the floor. A few shirts and pairs of pants are stuffed into it. I didn't bother folding them. I'm not even sure what I grabbed.

I shrug, chuckling to myself again. There doesn't seem to be anything left to do except laugh. If I don't laugh, I'll start crying, and I'm not ready to cry yet. "I don't even know. I just came up here and started packing. It's not like I have anywhere to go."

I stormed up the stairs as soon as I came inside, or at least I think I did. The minutes after I left Iz standing out on the stoop are a blur. The upstairs hallway is packed with people standing around to chat and drink, but I found Iz's room empty. My body was on autopilot at that point, and when I saw my suitcase, I started filling it with anything I could grab.

"I just want to get out of here," I tell Hope.

"I take it the talk was a disaster?"

I bark out another laugh. "Yeah. Yeah, you could say that."

I make my way over to Iz's bed and sit down on the edge, tapping my empty cup against one of my knees. The music is so loud I can feel the bass pounding through the floor under my feet.

"You know, if you really don't want to stay here tonight, you could crash at my girlfriend's place." Hope comes over to join me on the mattress. "She had to work tonight, so she skipped the party. I was gonna head over there myself pretty soon. You could come with me. I'm not gonna lie; the couch isn't fantastic, but I'm sure it's no problem for you to crash there."

I turn to face her. "Really?"

She nods and smiles. "Yeah. Becca won't care, and her roommates are super chill."

A trickle of relief floods through me. "Wow, you're like

my guardian angel this weekend. Where did you even come from?"

She shrugs. "I do what I can. Honestly, Becca and I went through hell and back before we got together last semester. I know what it's like to have your whole love life implode. It's nice to be able to be there for someone going through kind of the same thing. It's got to suck to be stuck away from home while you're dealing with this."

"Ughhh." I let my shoulders slump. "I still have one whole night left after this. I don't know if I can afford to change my flights."

"Well, the offer stands."

I pause to think about it, but there's not much of a debate to be had. I feel weird for crashing at a stranger's house, but my only other option is to sit in this bedroom and wait for the party to die down before facing Iz. I don't even know if the living room here will be inhabitable tonight, and there's no way Iz and I can share a bed.

Not after what I said.

Not after what they *didn't* say.

I squeeze my cup so hard it crumples in my fist. I'm not letting myself think about any of it. Not yet. If I replay any part of that conversation in my mind, I'm going to lose it right here in the middle of this party. I'm going to break down on the floor, scattered pieces of my heart strewn everywhere like a half-packed suitcase.

I'll start wondering if it was all worth it, and I can't let myself do that. I drew a line, and I need to stand my ground.

I need to be there for me, even if Iz can't be.

"Thank you." I nod at Hope. "That would be really great. I just need to pack a few more things."

Hope sweeps her arm out in a gesture for me to continue, and after a few minutes of packing with more than blind emotional turmoil to guide me, I've gathered up what I need and grabbed a few things from the bathroom. I stuff enough supplies for an overnighter into my shoulder bag, since there's already been enough drama tonight without me marching through the middle of the party carrying a suitcase.

I follow Hope down the stairs. My frozen feet have got most of their feeling back, and the addition of a fresh pair of socks helps. I pull my boots on in the entryway while Hope slips into her coat.

"It's not far," she shouts over the music. "I'm just going to tell Jane I'm heading out."

I tell myself not to look for Iz while she's gone, but I can't resist a sweeping glance around the living room. The sea of faces and waving arms are a blur as I try to make out the familiar shaggy brown pixie cut and striped button-down, but I don't see them anywhere. I hear their words from outside echo back to me as I keep looking.

I can't.

That's all they could say to me: I can't.

I told them I'm in love with them, and they said, 'I can't.'

"You ready?" Hope shouts, materializing from the crowd in front of me.

I turn away from the party and nod.

Hope leads the way outside, with me swinging my shoulder bag on behind her. The cold isn't as bad now that I'm actually dressed for winter. We're quiet as we trudge up the sidewalk. We head in the same direction we did for our walk before Hope makes a turn onto a street with a few big trees lining the road. Their branches cast jagged shadows over us as we pass underneath.

"Oh shit, it's almost one in the morning," Hope says

after pulling her phone out of her coat pocket. "Becca might be in bed already."

"Oh." I shift my bag's straps up farther on my shoulder. "I could go back? I don't want to be a bother."

She waves me off. "Don't worry about it. Let me text her and see if she replies."

We go back to walking in silence, and it gives me a very unwanted opportunity to return to my thoughts. Every second that passes gives my subconscious a chance to soak up another few drops of reality. That's as much as I can handle at a time, but bit by bit, I'm absorbing everything tonight meant.

I might have just lost my best friend.

Hope laughs as she taps at her screen. "Surprisingly, she is awake. She got caught up in a Netflix binge. Oh, and she says it's totally fine for you to spend the night."

A few of the smaller knots in stomach loosen. "Oh, awesome. I was really hoping I wouldn't have to go back."

We both chuckle and then lapse into silence. I can feel her eyes on me as I stare straight ahead. She inhales like she's about to ask me something, but I beat her to it.

"So, um, how long have you and Becca been dating?"

I glance to the side and see she's still watching me like she's debating asking me something more serious instead, but after a moment, she shrugs. "We officially got together in November, at the end of the lacrosse season."

"Right, right. Iz told me that."

I wince at my own words, and it really starts to hit me then: what not having Iz in my life would mean. I start so many sentences with 'Iz told me' or 'This one time with Iz' or 'Iz and I.' Sometimes I feel like something hasn't really happened to me until I've shared it with Iz. They're part of how I process the world.

I know I can be on my own. I know that after I

crumble and stand back up, I'll still be able to live my life, but I don't *want* a life without them. They're the colour in my skies. They're the comfort and the laughter and the place I go to heal. They're my person.

"This is it!" Hope's voice pulls me out of my thoughts. We've just approached a giant, old-fashioned three-storey house with a huge wraparound porch and the tallest, gnarliest tree on the street growing in the front yard.

My jaw drops. "She lives *here*?"

Hope laughs. "It's been divided up into a bunch of units. The whole place is rented by students. Even Becca doesn't know how many people live there in total. She shares the top floor with two roommates."

Hope stops in the middle of the path that leads to the porch and looks up to the top of the house, lifting her hand in a wave. I follow her gaze and spot one of the top floor windows with the lights still on inside. The white lace curtains have been pushed aside, and there's a girl with red hair waving down at us.

She disappears a second later, and by the time we make it onto the porch and up to the wooden door with a big old-fashioned handle, it's already swinging open to reveal the same girl.

She's gorgeous, but in a sharp, intimidating way, like a hawk or an eagle. Even in a pair of plaid pajama bottoms and UNS hoodie, she gives off an air of command, like anyone in her immediate vicinity would have no choice but to drop into a set of push-ups if she ordered it.

I can definitely understand how she scored the team captain role.

"Hey, babe." Hope steps forward to kiss her on the cheek, and some of the sharpness melts from Becca's face. If I wasn't feeling so unenthused about the concept of love in general at the moment, I'd find it super cute.

"All done partying?" Becca asks. "I thought you guys would be going until sunrise."

"It was kind of lame, to be honest," Hope answers. "There were way too many people. All anyone could really do was stand around."

Becca makes space for us to move into the entryway. The only light is coming from somewhere up the stairs, but I can make out the high arch of the ceiling and an array of winter boots stored on, around, and under a three-tiered rack. The rug under our feet is caked with salt stains from so many people coming in and out of the house.

"I'm Becca, by the way." She offers me her hand, and her grip is as firm and authoritative as everything else about her seems to be.

"Marina. Thanks so much for letting me come over, by the way. I know it's kind of, um, weird."

Becca shrugs. "Hope loves talking to strangers. I knew it was only a matter of time before she tried to bring one home to live with us."

"Hey!" Hope elbows her in the thigh while bending over to take her boots off.

"And besides," Becca continues, reaching down to pet Hope's head, "you're not a stranger. You're a friend of a friend."

If we're even friends anymore.

"She's *my* friend!" Hope straightens up and beams at me, interrupting my personal pity party. "We're basically BFFs."

It does feel good to have a friend in all this. I force myself to give what I hope isn't a totally miserable excuse for a smile. "Would that be BBFFs?"

Becca throws her head back and laughs. Her laugh is lighter than I would have expected, more carefree and open than the rest of her. "That was a good one. You've earned entrance into the apartment."

We all trudge up the stairs. These ones are almost as creaky as the staircase in the Babe Cave. The unit Becca lets us into is dark except for the light over the stove. The kitchen and living room make up one big, conjoined space, and there's a narrow hallway with a few doors leading off to one side. I can smell a hint of sesame oil and teriyaki in the air, like someone had stir fry for dinner. My stomach growls, and I try not to think about how long it's been since I ate.

"I'll get you set up, Marina," Becca says in a voice just above a murmur.

I do as much as I can to help as she and Hope get the couch decked out with blankets and pillows and prepare some towels for me.

"Feel free to take a shower tonight if you want," Becca tells me as she hands me the striped blue and white towels, "and grab whatever you want out of the fridge."

"Oh, thanks." I resist the urge to fist pump as my stomach keeps gurgling to remind me it's in desperate need of filling.

"I am fucking starving," Hope says, loud enough that Becca makes a shushing motion. She continues in a quieter voice. "Marina, do you want a midnight snack?"

"Sure!" I answer, only somewhat managing not to sound desperate.

She's already heading into the kitchen. She hunts around in the fridge for a few seconds before pulling out a Tupperware. "Is this stir fry?"

Becca nods beside me. "Leftovers. You guys can have them. Actually, heat the whole thing up. I want some too."

Fifteen minutes later, we're all scraping the last of the food off our plates as quietly as we can while Hope and

Becca—but mostly Hope—drag the story of what happened tonight out of me question by question. The longer we talk, the easier it is to share, and the more I realize I need to get this out.

"That's all they said?" Becca asks.

I nod. We've reached the point in the recounting where I left Iz standing on the stoop and went back inside. "Yep. That's all they said."

"Shit." Hope sets her plate down on the small kitchen table we're all sitting around. "I really thought they'd say *something*. It's just so clear they have feelings for you. I get being scared, but you're their best friend. You'd think they could come to you with that fear."

I slump back in my chair. "I'm not sure. Maybe I have it wrong. I can't deny there have been moments when we've clearly been mutually attracted to each other, but that just happens between friends sometimes, right? Maybe it's nothing more. Maybe I read too much into it. Maybe *I* don't even feel the way I think I do."

Becca and Hope don't even bother to hide their doubt about that one. They both stare at me like I've just announced I believe the earth is flat.

I sigh. "Okay, so that's bullshit. It's just..."

It's just easier to tell myself I made it all up. It's easier to put myself in the wrong than to admit how much Iz hurt me.

"I think you know how you feel," Becca says slowly, "and I think you know how Iz feels. I think maybe they're just...not ready. When dating someone also means facing some of your worst fears about yourself, there's a lot you have to battle through before you're actually ready to do the dating. You kind of have to hit rock bottom first to even get a clear look at the whole picture."

Hope's staring at her with the softest expression I've

ever seen on her face. She grips Becca's forearm where it's resting on the table. "Is that what it was like for you? With us?"

Becca nods. "Yeah, that was exactly it. I was so scared, but almost losing my shot with you made me realize how much scarier *that* was. In the end, I really needed you to tell me I wasn't stepping up enough. I needed you to draw that line so I could figure out how to jump over it."

"Mhmm." Hope laces her fingers through Becca's and turns to me. "And I needed to figure out what I could take and what I couldn't. I needed to tell myself what I was worth."

I cough to clear the lump that forms in my throat as I watch the two of them sitting there like the picture of queer bliss. Just two days ago, I thought that's where I might be now.

"Wow, you guys," I say, doing my best to downplay the shake in my voice, "I feel like I'm facilitating an Oprah interview."

Becca chuckles, and Hope starts to belly laugh before Becca leans over and nips her on the shoulder to urge her to be quiet. I see Hope's eyes flare, and I decide I'd better wrap this up before the two of them go from being cute to being exhibitionists.

"Thank you, though," I add. "That helps."

It does help. I don't have much hope left for a happy ending, but I know I couldn't have been happy in the friendship as it was. Like Hope said, I need to know my worth, and I'm worth more than spending my life waiting for someone else to step up.

I just wish I felt more triumphant about it all. Every breath I take feels like it's getting closer and closer to turning into a sob.

"Well, we better clean up and get to bed," Becca says

as she lifts her arms above her head in a stretch. "We've got that morning jog to go on, Hope."

Hope groans. "Oh my god, you're not seriously still thinking about doing that are you? We can go to the gym in the afternoon."

"It's on my schedule," Becca protests. "Sunday is a jogging day."

"I'm surrounded by jocks," I tease them as I start gathering up the plates.

We get everything put away, and Hope and Becca are both yawning by the time they close the bedroom door, but I'm wide awake. I take Becca up on the offer to use the shower and spend a few minutes cleaning the last of the makeup off my face.

I stare at myself in the mirror when I'm done, my damp hair laying flat against my bare shoulders and my body naked except for the towel wrapped around my waist. I look at the freckles dotting my cheeks, the constellations of beauty marks on my stomach and chest, the curves of my hips under the towel.

It took a long time for me to learn to be happy with everything I see when I look at myself, but I got there.

"I'm sorry," I say to the girl in the mirror. "I'm sorry I was mean to you tonight."

It's a habit I got into whenever I think something negative about my body: I apologize just like I would for saying the same thing to somebody else. I say sorry for telling myself people are laughing at me. I say sorry for telling myself I should hide and stay out of sight. I say sorry for telling myself I'm awkward and unwanted.

I know what I'm worth. I know what my love is worth, and I can't keep pouring it into someone who isn't ready to do anything except pour it right back out.

After I've slipped my pajamas on and snuggled in

under the blankets on the couch, I reach for my phone on the coffee table. The same lock screen I've had for years greets me when I click the power button: Iz and I as dorky little kids in a laundry basket.

I open up my photo gallery and scroll through it. In between all the shots of pretty flowers I've seen, photogenic food I've made or ordered, roomie wine night selfies with Alexis, and funny photos of my family back home, there are pictures of me and Iz. The two of us are woven through the story of my life like a golden thread snaking through a multi-coloured tapestry.

There are pictures of us hanging out in Toronto, selfies and video clips from our visits at each other's schools, and screenshots of Iz doing ridiculous things like trying on three pairs of sunglasses at once or trying to balance as many gummy bears as possible on their face during our video calls.

I pause on that last one and chuckle. I remember shrieking and taking the screenshot when they started licking the gummy bears to get them to stick. I'd been feeling down about getting a lower grade than I expected on an essay, and Iz only needed a pack of gummy bears to make me forget all about it.

A pang of loss so intense it makes my breath hitch slams into my body, and the photo gets blurry as my eyes fill with tears.

I dump the phone back on the table and smush a pillow over my face as the first sob finally forces its way out of me.

I did the right thing.

I repeat it to myself like a mantra as I curl up on my side, the pillow still muffling the sounds I'm making.

I did what I had to.

I believe it, but that doesn't make it hurt any less.

10

Iz

I've never done any drugs except trying weed a couple times, but I imagine this must be what a bad trip feels like. The floor lurches under my feet, and all the faces crowded around me are a distorted blur as I stumble my way through the party.

The music throbs and pulses in my head like a rhythmic migraine, and by the time I reach the kitchen, I just want to sit down on the floor with my head between my knees and my hands over my ears.

Instead, I walk straight past all the people crowded around the table and leaning against the tiny counter without answering their shouts or waves. I don't have to ask the guy propped against the fridge to move; he takes one look at me and steps aside.

The inside of the fridge looks like it's been raided by bandits, but in true birthday miracle fashion, there's a bottle of white wine with at least a glass left inside.

I'm not much of a wine person, but I still grab the bottle and polish the tangy liquid off in a few sips without bothering to look for a cup.

I make a face and groan as I dump the empty bottle in the recycling bin. "*Dios*, that tastes like vinegar."

The few people close enough to hear me all laugh, but I don't join in. Someone wishes me a happy birthday, but I just nod in the direction of their voice as I head back out of the kitchen.

If I stop moving, I'll start thinking, and I don't want to think right now. Panic is clawing at the edges of my mind, and it's going to rip me up if I let it. Marina can't have left any more than ten minutes ago, but it feels like I've been caught in a time warp ever since. Hours could have passed me by. Everything has been a blur since Hope came and told me she was taking Marina to Becca's tonight.

I edge my way back across the living room, heading for the stairs. I notice the piñata shaped like a running shoe has been smashed open. I think I remember Jane taking charge and poking a hole in the bottom with the end of a broom since there are way too many people in here for us to be swinging a stick around, but all my memories of tonight are already going foggy. The beer is catching up with me, and I can still feel the warmth of the wine settling in my stomach.

I pass under the cardboard piñata remnants still dangling from the ceiling and finally get to the edge of the staircase. A few people slap me on the back or raise their drinks at me as I clear a path through everyone loitering on the steps.

I blink my eyes into focus and scan for Jane or Paulina among all the faces. I want this party over, and I need their help to do it. I reach inside my pockets and then remember I still haven't found my damn phone.

The upstairs hallway is less crowded than the living room. Most of the people up here are actually trying to have conversations. I get to my door and brace to find some couple making out on my bed or a bunch of hockey guys trying to hotbox the room, but there's no one inside. I shut the door behind me and lunge for my window, cracking it open and taking a few deep gulps of the frigid air that seeps into the overheated house.

After a few more breaths, I sit down on the edge of my bed and prop my head in my hands.

I think I'm in love with you, Iz.

She just said it. Just like that. She laid it all on the line, and I let her walk away. I fucking *choked*. I choked on every what-if and maybe, every fear and worry and burning recognition that she was right about it all.

I can't remember the last time I went after a girl I genuinely thought things might work out with. I'm always braced for it to end as soon as it starts, and as much as it sucks to admit it, there's a certain comfort in that.

If I know it's going to happen, it doesn't hurt as much. It doesn't hurt like the first time.

I stop rubbing circles into my temples and sit up straight. I've been drumming my heels against the floor without realizing it, and the room gets quieter when my Jordans are no longer tapping out a frantic rhythm. My body is still in flight response, urging me to move and take action.

I look around and spot an old lacrosse ball sitting on my desk. I get up to grab it and then sit back down on the bed. My hands start up the same routine I use to help me study for chemistry tests: bouncing the ball on the floor to make it rebound off the wall and then bounce back to the bed. I usually use each beat of the lacrosse ball to reel off part of a formula, but tonight I just number them.

One bounce.
Two bounce.
Three bounce.

Four bounce.

I've always been able to rely on lacrosse. No two games are the same, but there are parts of them that are always predictable. I'm far from being the team's MVP, but I'm good at remembering plays and putting them into action. I like the satisfaction of seeing something we've all drilled a thousand times at practice play out at breakneck speed during a game. There's something exhilarating about seeing every detail fall into place.

Thirteen bounce.

Fourteen bounce.

Fifteen bounce.

Of course, there are always those games that go totally off the rails. Sometimes we lose a guaranteed win, and sometimes we win a guaranteed loss. We adapt and keep going. We make new patterns and plans. We grow.

I'm usually not the one involved in those decisions. The coach and captain take care of that.

"Iz?"

I hold onto the ball the next time it bounces into my hands and turn to look at the door. Olivia's head is peeking around the edge.

"Can I come in?"

I nod. "Yeah. For sure."

I want to say no, but I haven't been great to her tonight. I'm the one who invited her here, and I've walked out of two different conversations with her to go looking for Marina. I know I'm giving off major mixed signals, and even though an especially salty part of me wants to think she deserves it, I'm not going to keep putting someone through that.

After closing the door behind her, she crosses the room to sit down next to me, leaving a couple feet between us. She's still close enough for me to smell the coconut body lotion I remember from when we were seeing each other, but it doesn't make me feel anything except a dull flicker of familiarity, like flipping through yearbook pages filled with people you used to know.

It's nothing like catching the scent of Marina's jasmine shampoo or the smell of her skin on my sheets.

I'm about to clear the air and let Olivia know nothing's going to happen between us, but she beats me to it.

"I probably should have been honest with you when I said I would come to the party," she says as she fiddles with the end of one of her braids. "I know I was kind of flirty, but I don't think it's a good idea for us to hook up again."

"Me neither." I nod, and in the moment of silence that follows, I blurt out the first thing on my mind. "I, um, I'm sorry if I was ever, like...clingy...with you."

My voice is flat, but I still cringe as I say it. I cringe at what she must think of me. The party downstairs isn't as loud now, but the thump of the bass still fills the silence between us. I stare down at the ball in my hands as I roll it between my palms.

"Iz."

I keep rolling the ball, waiting for the rest.

"Iz, look at me."

When I lift my head, I find her watching me with her eyebrows all wrinkled like she has no idea what I'm talking about.

"I don't know what you think you have to say sorry about," she says slowly, "but I came up here to apologize to *you*."

I blink. "About...what?"

"For being dishonest with you." She looks down at her lap and runs her palms along the thighs of her jeans. "I kind of used you, and it was really shitty of me. I pretended I didn't know what I was doing, but now I see that I did. I...I really liked hanging out with you. A lot. I liked all the stuff we did together. It really meant something to me, but I'm just...not in a place where I'm ready for a relationship, and instead of telling you that, I went along with things until I couldn't anymore and then justified brushing you off by telling myself it was only ever casual anyways."

The ball drops out of my hands and thuds on the floor.

"I...wow." I stare down at the ground between my feet, shaking my head. "I mean...*what*? You mean that? All of that?"

"Yeah." She gives me a small smile laced with regret. "I really do."

My head is spinning again. "I thought...I thought I just read it all wrong. I thought I fucked up and misinterpreted everything and made you think I was some clingy freak who couldn't handle casual."

"Iz..." She crossed her arms over her stomach as her face twists with pain. "God, I'm the one who fucked up. You must have felt crazy, and it's all my fault. I just couldn't step up and be honest. I'm so, so sorry."

I tilt my head, still trying to figure this out.

"So you don't think I'm...too much?"

"What? Of course not. Iz, anyone would be lucky to be your girlfriend. We weren't even officially dating, and you made me feel like a queen. You're not too much at all."

I sit there gawking at her for so long she shifts on the bed and lets out a nervous laugh. I know I should come up with an answer, but I feel like I'm caught up in working out a crazily complicated chemistry formula. My mouth is hanging open like a cartoon, and my brain is too busy adding up all the facts to do anything about my slack jaw.

"Okay, listen..." The ball has come to rest just a few inches from one of Olivia's feet. She leans forward to grab it and starts copying my bouncing routine. "I haven't officially dated anyone since my parents got divorced. I'm scared to be in love and have it fall apart like that, so I just...don't let myself go far enough to feel those things. I know it's fucked up, but it's easier that way. Except being with you...Being with you made me realize how much I've been missing out on, and how much I've been hurting myself. I hurt you too. That's when I knew I needed to do something about it. I, uh, I found a counsellor."

Her voice falters, and her eyes stay glued to the ball as it bounces against the floor, the wall, and then back into her hands.

"That's amazing, Olivia. You don't have to be embarrassed about that."

She bobs her head in a few nervous nods. "Thanks. I just, um...like I'm not trying to get us together or anything. I need to be with myself for a while. It's just important to me that you know what was going on and that I'm sorry."

"Well...thank you." I keep my gaze trained on the ball too. "That really means a lot."

It means more than I can understand in this moment, but I'm grateful. Her words have straightened out something inside me, something that feels like it's been crooked for years. It's like setting a bone back in place: so uncomfortable you want to scream and so unfamiliar you don't know how to move your own body, but ultimately for the best.

"I get being scared," I tell her. "We all do things we regret when we're scared or hurting."

She glances at me before catching the ball. "Your friend, the girl who's visiting. You have a thing with her, right?"

I jerk in surprise. "Huh?"

The corner of her mouth lifts. "Yeah, I saw that. You

totally do. You made me feel good, Iz, but you never looked at me like I saw you watching her."

I can feel my cheeks getting hot. "She's...we're..."

"Yeah, I thought so." Olivia's smile widens before fading. "Are you two fighting?"

"We..."

'Fight' doesn't seem like the right word for what happened tonight, but I guess that's what it was.

"Kind of, yeah, I guess," I stammer. "I don't even know if we'll be friends anymore after this."

She catches the ball again and then drops it in my lap, nodding for me to start throwing. We begin a new pattern, trading off catches each time the ball rebounds from the wall.

"I don't know anything about it," Olivia says, "but maybe it's like you said to me: we all do things we regret when we're scared."

I let out a shaky breath. "I just don't know if I'm ready to stop being scared yet."

"So tell her that."

She laughs at what I'm sure is my totally terrified expression.

"I'm really on the truth train lately," she adds. "Honesty is the way to go, even if it's messy."

"But what if it's *really* messy?"

She lifts an eyebrow. "As opposed to how it is now?"

Even I have to laugh at that one. "Okay, fair point."

She throws a little too hard, and the ball comes speeding back to us way too high in the air. I push up onto my feet just in time and grab it with one hand before it can slam into the wall behind us.

Olivia purses her lips like she's impressed. "Damn, Iz. Nice catch."

I sit back down and lift my arm to throw again, but she gets to her feet instead.

"I think I'd better go home now. I really mean it, though. I'm sorry. For everything."

She doesn't break eye contact as she says it, and that more than anything lets me know she means it. I see the shame in her expression, but I also see the promise to do better for whoever comes after me.

"Thank you. Apology totally accepted."

She nods. "Goodnight, Iz."

"Goodnight, Olivia."

She stops with her hand on the doorknob and looks back. "Oh, and happy birthday."

I almost start laughing at how weird that sounds. I totally forgot it was my birthday.

I flop down on my back as soon as she leaves, the lacrosse ball still clutched in one of my hands. I stare at the ring of light my bedside lamp casts on the ceiling, and it doesn't take long before I'm picturing Marina's face.

I've never seen her look as hurt as she did tonight.

I'm the one who did that to her.

I rub my eyes and then get up to put the ball back on my desk. That's when I notice the black rectangle poking out from under a stray course syllabus.

"Oh fuck yes!" I shout as I shift the paper aside to reveal my missing phone.

I have a few texts from people wishing me happy birthday and a couple from Jane asking where I am. I type out a reply as I wander back over to my bed and collapse onto my back again.

After a few minutes of scrolling through the messages, I end up opening my gallery. The last photo I took was a selfie of me and Marina on the way here from the airport. The light from the bus window behind us creates a halo effect around our heads and shoulders. Our cheeks are just a couple inches apart, and she's blurry from laughing at the cross-eyed face I'm making.

I made her smile like that. Just two days ago, we were laughing so hard our stomachs hurt.

I keep scrolling, looking through picture after picture of the two of us: making gingerbread houses with her family, posing with one of my cousins from Colombia on Christmas Eve, eating popsicles during summer break, hanging out in the library on one of my visits to Kingston, getting ready for a night out with Hope.

In every single one of them, she's laughing and smiling beside me.

I love making her laugh. It's one of my favourite, favourite things.

I want to do it again. I want to do it over and over again for the rest of my life, and maybe that is terrifying, but it's also beautiful. It takes my breath away and fills me up all at the same time.

I think I might be in love with you, Iz.

Haven't I been wishing for someone to say that to me? Haven't I been hoping to hear it from every single girl I've dated?

Now those words are coming from my favourite person in the world, the person who's had my back through every challenge I've ever faced, and I'm too fucking scared to say anything in return.

I think about what Olivia told me tonight. I thought *I* was the problem, but maybe she and Marina are right. Maybe I'm not too much. Maybe I've just been giving my love to people who aren't ready to take it.

Maybe Marina's going through the same thing with me.

What would it take to be ready?

What would it take to prove I am?

I sit up and start tossing the ball again, counting from the top.

One bounce.

Two bounce.

Three bounce.

I think about those questions. I sit there tossing and counting and thinking about them for a long, long time.

11

Iz

I wake up with a headache at what has to be the crack of dawn. I forgot to cover my window last night, and the piercing white light of one of those rare, clear coastal winter days shines straight into my eyes and pulls me out of sleep.

"Bright," I croak as I throw my arm over my face. "So bright."

It's too late to fall back asleep. The glow of the room seeps in around the edges of my arm like it's taunting me.

"*Mierdaaaaa*," I rasp as I fling the covers off me and sit up.

My head rushes, and little dots cover my vision for a few seconds. I look around the room after they fade away, waiting for something to reveal why there's a pit of nerves starting to twist and churn in my stomach like a nest of snakes.

That's when I spot the page of notes scribbled on the back of a syllabus sitting on my bedside table. It all comes flooding back: the party, Olivia, Marina.

Marina.

I grab the paper and scan my sloppy handwriting. There's a column labelled 'Things Marina Likes' and another called 'Ideas.' I must have been in a worse state than I thought last night; my writing is messy at the best of times, but now it's a struggle for even me to make out the words.

One of the 'ideas' at the top of the column is circled several times. It's one of the easier bullet points to decipher. I read the words over a few times. They don't do anything to ease the twisting in my stomach or the sweat breaking out on the back of my neck, but I feel something else pumping through my veins besides stress and regret.

I have purpose. I have a direction to take, and I might not know where exactly I'll end up, but I'm not helpless anymore. I'm scared, but I'm not stuck.

My bare feet land on the chilly hardwood floor. I pull a pair of oversized socks on and head into the hallway in some boxers and a giant Lobsters t-shirt. I can still smell the sticky-sweet tang of beer in the air. The bathroom looks like it was used by a crowd of people who've never operated a sink before; soap and water speckles are splashed almost up to the ceiling. The singed remains of a joint are sitting on the windowsill, along with a few Solo cups.

It's like we got visited by the Easter bunny's wild frat boy of a younger brother.

I brush my teeth as fast as I can, avoiding looking at my drained, half-dead face as much as possible. I head downstairs and find the trail of Solo cups continues all the way into the living room and kitchen. I can't spot any broken furniture, but the floors are a mess.

The smell is so bad I crack a few windows open despite the cold outside. The longer I'm awake, the more the mix of nerves and determination intensifies. Soon it's like a drum pounding along in time with my heart, louder and stronger than the parts of me that want to shrink and go back.

There is no going back. After last night, there is only room to go forward.

Eating is the last thing on my mind, but I know it's probably a good idea given everything I'll need to get done today. Our cupboards have been ravaged by hungry drunk people, but I find the box of my favourite crackers untouched and carry them back up to my room.

Hope's door is open, giving me a view of her empty bed, but both Jane and Paulina seem to be home. The hallway creaks when I reach my own door. I head inside and unplug my phone's charger before checking the time.

It's only five past eight. I sit on the edge of my bed and shovel a few crackers into my mouth, chewing so fast I'm sure I look like a manic squirrel. I feel like a manic squirrel. I need to *move*. I need to put my probably insane plan into action, but first I need my friends, which means waiting for them to wake up.

I grab the biggest chemistry textbook I own in the hopes it will lull my brain into a state where every passing minute doesn't feel excruciatingly long, but I can only digest a few words at a time before I'm back to thinking about how the rest of today might go.

How Marina will look when I see her, what I'll say to her, what she'll say to me.

She could tell me to go to hell. She could tell me she never wants to see me again. She could show up at the door here before I have a chance to go to her, grab her suitcase from where it's tucked into the corner in my room, and get on a plane back to Kingston.

I pull up our text conversation on my phone and stare

at the message box. There are so many things I want her to hear, but they all seem best to say in person.

I groan and reach for my textbook again, settling back against my headboard and propping it on my chest. I flip to the periodic table in the index and quiz myself on the elements. At this point they're all branded into my memory for life, so it's not much of a distraction.

By a quarter past nine, I feel like I'm about to explode. My hands and feet are twitching with the need to get moving, and I literally jump to my feet when I hear the floor outside my door creak. I poke my head into the hallway and spot the back of a guy without a shirt on just before he shuts himself in the bathroom.

At least someone had a good night.

Paulina's conquest has left her door open. Her blackout curtains are still drawn, but I can make out the shape of her under the blankets from here. I take a few steps into the hallway.

"Paulina," I whisper, "are you awake?"

She doesn't answer. I move closer, and the floorboards creak.

"Yo, Paulina," I try again, louder this time. "You up?"

She murmurs something in a sleepy voice, and I take that as enough of an invitation to pad into her room. I crawl onto the empty side of the bed like an overexcited kid on Christmas morning. She mutters again, the words so slurred I can't tell what she's saying. She's lying on her side, facing away from me. I can't see much more of her besides a mass of blonde hair.

"Uh, what?" I whisper.

"I said, wow I've never done that position before." Her voice is still groggy as her fingertips appear over the edge of the comforter and inch the blankets away from her face.

"What's that called? Reverse cowgirl? We should do that again sometime."

I try so hard to hold my laugh back I start choking.

"Uh, yeah," I splutter. "I'm sure he'd love to go for round two."

She rolls over and yanks the blankets down far enough for me to realize she's not wearing a shirt. Her eyes are narrowed to slits.

"*Iz?*" she demands, her voice cracking like a teenaged boy's. "What the hell are you doing in my bed?"

"Uh, yeah, about that. I have a question for you."

"Why didn't you just knock on my door like a normal person?"

I sit up on my knees, bouncing a little on the mattress. "It's still early. I didn't want to wake you up."

"Well I'm very awake now."

"Yes, I see that. Do you know anyone with a car? I mean, preferably a moped, but a car works too."

She squints for another few seconds and then wiggles her hand out to rub her eyes while the other one holds the blankets to her chest. "It is way too early for this. Why the fuck do you need a moped?"

"I'm making a grand romantic gesture."

She squints at me as she rubs her forehead. "To who?"

"Marina. I think I might be in love with her."

I wait for my nerves to go haywire, for the bottom of my stomach to drop while my breath morphs into frantic gasps, but none of that happens. As soon as the words leave my mouth, I feel my lips stretching into a smile so wide it hurts my cheeks.

I'm in love with Marina.

It's that 'aha' moment at the end of a chemistry experiment, when the reaction fizzles out and you're left with the final result. All the questions are gone. There's only certainty as you marvel at the way a few chemicals can come together to make something new and strong.

It's more than chemistry; it's alchemy. The warmth spreading in my chest is pure gold.

I can do this.

"Oh." Paulina sits up a little straighter, still squinting at me. "*Oh.*"

I watch her start to smile too, the sleepiness clearing from her eyes as they spark with excitement.

"Yeah." I hold back the urge to start jumping on the bed like a toddler. "I have to tell her, but I have to make it special. Things...did not go well last night."

Now Paulina's grin is getting smug. "I knew you two were gonna end up together."

"That's the thing, though. We're not together. Not yet. So I need a moped."

She tilts her head to the side. "That part I don't follow."

"It's—"

My explanation gets caught off by the sound of the floor creaking under someone's footsteps.

"Uh, hey. Is this...what I think it is?"

I look over and see the guy Paulina apparently rode like a cowgirl—in reverse—standing in the bedroom doorway, staring at us with his eyes bulging out of his head.

"I'm like, so down," he continues. He's trying to sound casual, but his voice squeaks at the end of his sentence. "I mean, even if you just want me to watch, I—"

"Aaaand that's my cue to leave." I get to my feet just as he starts walking into the room.

He looks back and forth between Paulina and I like his dude brain hasn't caught up with the fact that he is not getting a threesome this morning.

"Wait, Iz." Paulina sits all the way up and almost

drops the blankets covering her chest, which doesn't seem to help clear our hopeful visitor's head. "I want to help! Just give me a few minutes, and I'll meet you downstairs."

"It's okay if you're busy. I—"

She shakes her head, fully awake and buzzing with almost as much excitement as me now. "No no no. We need to make this happen. I'll be right there."

"Okay." I clap my hands together. "Okay. Right. Yes. Let's do this!"

I turn to charge out the door, and that's when we all notice Jane standing in the hallway, wearing a decrepit bathrobe over an oversized UNS Athletics t-shirt that goes all the way to her knees. Her hair is rumpled, and she's squinting at us like even the dim light of the hallway is too much for her at this hour.

"Do I even want to know what's going on in there?" she asks, her voice hoarse.

"Iz is in love with Marina!" Paulina shouts. "We're going to make a grand romantic gesture!"

"Oh." Jane blinks a few times and then nods. "Let me make some coffee."

The guy beside me clears his throat as Jane heads for the bathroom. "So...this isn't what I think it is?"

I pat him on the shoulder. "No, my dude. No, it is not."

He nods a few times, his forehead creased like he's processing some life-changing information. "Should I...go?"

"I had a lovely time last night." Paulina manages to keep the blanket in place as she flips her hair over shoulder and bats her eyes at him. "You can stay for coffee if you want."

"Especially if you know someone with a moped," I joke, "or at least a car."

He blinks and looks between the two of us. "Uh, I don't know about mopeds, but I have a car at my place."

―――

"YOU'RE sure it's okay if I drive it?"

I step back from attaching the final streamer to the back of the car. The rusty, navy blue Subaru looks like it might be older than me. It has enough dents and scratches to imply it's seen some serious shit, and every wheeze the engine made while coming up our street sounded like it might be the car's dying breath, but it's here and it's a car. That's all I need.

"Yeah, for sure. Just don't crash it."

Bradley, as I've learned the guy from Paulina's bedroom is called, is standing on the sidewalk in front of the Babe Cave next to her and Jane. After he caught up with the fact that a ménage was not in his future, he turned into a pretty sweet and helpful dude—which makes me feel less guilty about Paulina basically pimping herself out to get us this car. She asked him out as we all sat sipping coffee in the kitchen, which seemed to solidify the car sharing plan.

"We're not going to go far, and I'll have it back to you by the end of the day."

He nods. "Yeah, for sure. You can even park it here tonight if you want."

Jane comes over to clap me on the shoulder. "Good luck, Izzo. Hope just texted to say Marina is still at Becca's place."

Pulling this together has been a real team effort. Hope is in on the plan, and she's been making sure Marina doesn't do anything drastic like head for the airport. Paulina and Jane helped me find all the right decorations for the car, and even Bradley pitched in with the decorating.

Streamers in the colours of the Italian flag are taped to the back of the car, and there's a sign that says 'Rome or bust' stretched across the trunk. We printed out pictures of mopeds to stick to the doors, and the passenger's side seat has a plastic tiara crowning the headrest over a paper sign that says 'Reserved for her Royal Highness.'

An actual moped would have been better, but considering it's winter in Halifax, I think we did a pretty damn good job paying tribute to the Audrey Hepburn classic, *Roman Holiday*.

AKA Marina's favourite movie of all time.

When we were kids, Marina would pretend she was Princess Ann from the movie while I pulled her around in a wagon that was supposed to be our getaway vehicle in Rome. I'd trudge through her backyard while we imagined running away from all the people trying to get her back to her royal duties. Sometimes I'd jump in the wagon with her, and we'd eat the cheese slices and grapes we packed for the adventure. I'd set her plate up for her and do gallant things like kissing her hand.

It was very fucking gay.

I smile to myself as I think back on it. I've been doing that a lot in the couple hours we've spent setting everything up. I keep thinking back on the past, watching it all click into place.

I've been in love with her this whole time, and as crazy as it is to say it, I think I always knew. I tried to push it away, but I can't push away who I am, and so much of me is because of her.

"Thank you, Jane. Thank you, all of you. I know this has been, uh, a weird day so far, but just...thanks." I take a deep breath and walk over to the driver's side door. "Okay, here I go."

I smooth down the front of the shirt I'm wearing: a black and white button-down I got during a thrifting session with Marina in Toronto a few years ago. I have a black blazer thrown on top, and my winter coat is waiting in the back seat of the car just in case. I'm going to feel like an idiot standing there all dressed up if this goes wrong, but Marina deserves the best of everything.

The group on the sidewalk waves as I get inside and put the key in the ignition. The engine splutters and then revs to life. I grip the steering wheel and ease the car away from the sidewalk.

My hands start shaking as I cruise through the neighbourhood. Almost every building around here is rented by students, and on a Sunday morning in winter, the sidewalks are all but abandoned. There's a weird smell coming out of the heating vent beside me that is not helping my nerves, so I turn it off despite how cold the air in the car is.

I turn onto Becca's street and slow down as the giant old building with a huge tree in the front yard come into view. I ease the car to a stop under its branches and kill the engine.

I should get out now. I should move, but instead I sit there shivering with one hand still gripping the wheel.

My brain knows this time is different, but my body can't help remembering how much waiting around for Sheila to show up as my prom date felt exactly like this: the jittery anticipation combined with the blissed out high of knowing things were finally coming together.

Only they weren't, and for the longest time, I thought that was all my fault. Sitting here now, it suddenly feels stupid and hasty to think one night and a few conversations could undo the truth I've attached myself to for years.

I'm too much.

This car is the perfect example. It's *so* much. I've tried too hard, just like all those girls reminded me time and time again. I put in way too much effort. I scare people off. I pour myself out when I should hold myself in.

I take a shaky breath and think back to last night, to Marina in the dark front yard with the glow of the pink lights shining on her face.

There's nothing wrong with you, Iz. You have so much love in you. I know you do. I think you're just scared to let it out.

Olivia told me the same thing: there's nothing wrong with me. I'm normal. It's not my fault.

Hearing it from both of them was like feeding an aching hunger I didn't know was there, but I know I won't be satisfied until I can hear it from myself.

"There's nothing wrong with me," I whisper.

I sound fragile, like whatever I'm holding onto could be snatched out of my hands at any second.

I try again, louder this time.

"There's nothing wrong with me."

My voice fills the car, but it's not enough. I grip the wheel hard enough to make my knuckles go white, and then I take a deep breath.

"THERE'S NOTHING WRONG WITH ME."

I say it so loud it blocks everything else out. I say it loud enough to make it true.

Then I get out of the car.

12

Marina

Hope comes back from grabbing a bowl of chips for us in the kitchen and joins me on the couch. I ask her if I should press play on the teen drama we've been bingeing on Netflix, but she shakes her head.

"I just have to send a few texts first, and then we can continue watching these sixteen year-olds act like everything is the end of the world."

I laugh and reach for some chips. Hope and Becca got up at an ungodly hour to do their run. Becca took off for a group study session after but told us to stay as long as we wanted.

I feel like that one friend who shows up at your house for a 'short' visit and then sticks around so long you have to start scheming up ways to kick them out, but Becca didn't seem bothered, and it's not like I have anywhere else to go. I looked into changing my flights this morning, but the adjustment fee is almost as much as the tickets.

My departure time isn't until tomorrow afternoon, but I don't mind spending the day at the airport. If I can swallow my pride and ask to crash on the couch here another night, the only time I'll need to see Iz is when I go pick up the rest of my stuff.

The thought is like the jab of a knife in my skin, poking and prodding at wounds that haven't had a chance to close over. A few hours of sleep didn't do me any good; I still feel as ragged and raw as I did after the fight last night.

The pain seeps deeper with every second that ticks by, but I still can't quite grasp the reality of it all. A world in which Iz and I aren't friends just doesn't make sense. It's all crooked and warped, just a bunch of sharp angles waiting for me to trip and fall. Being with Iz was getting too painful to handle, but at least it was familiar. Now I've stepped out of what I knew and into a dizzying maze. I can't go back, but I can't figure out how to go forward either.

Maybe it will come with time.

Maybe this what everyone goes through when they finally let go.

That doesn't make it any easier.

"Oh my god!"

Hope's shout and gasp pulls me back into the moment. She's still staring down at her phone.

"What is it? Is everything okay?"

I watch her for signs of distress, but after some furious typing, she looks up and squeals. "Wait one second!"

She jumps off the couch and sprints over to the kitchen, where there's a window facing the street below. She stands on her tiptoes and leans over the counter underneath the windowpane before squealing again.

"Okay, *what* is going on?"

I stand up and start walking over, but she whirls around and holds her palm up like a crossing guard.

"Stop right there, lady! No peeking. You need to go downstairs. Oh, and put your coat on too."

"Hope, what is happening?" Despite my confusion, my

heart is already going a mile a minute as she bounds over and grabs my shoulders to steer me to the door.

"You'll see soon enough." She deposits me in front of the apartment door before pulling my coat off its hook and tossing it my way. "Oh, and let me get your purse."

She's bouncing on the balls of her feet now, a giant grin taking over her whole face. There's a glint in her eyes that's giving off some strong I-am-either-excited-or-on-drugs vibes. I let out a nervous laugh as I pull my coat on. My fingertips have gone numb, and my stomach is churning yet again.

This has to be about Iz.

"Okay, go, go, go, go, go!" Hope shouts, taking hold of my shoulders again a millisecond after I've got my arms through my sleeves. "Tally ho!"

"Did you really just say *tally ho*?" I demand as she yanks the door open and hustles me onto the staircase.

"I have no idea where that came from," she says from behind me. "Now move, Miss Marina! Your future awaits!"

"My future?"

She doesn't bother answering as she hurries us both down the stairs so fast I almost trip over my own feet.

"Get your boots on!" she commands once we're on the ground floor. "I have a feeling you're going to want to go outside."

"You're really taking this whole mystery thing pretty far. Hey, wait!" I look up from where I'm bent over my boots and find her jogging back up the stairs. "You're not staying?"

She pauses, still bouncing in place as she shakes her head. "Trust me, you're gonna want some privacy. Although I mayyyy be watching from the window."

She takes off tearing up the staircase, leaving me blinking and confused as ever as I turn to face the front door. The old-fashioned hunk of wood and stained-glass seems to loom in front of me like a portal into potential doom.

I hold my breath, reach for the tarnished handle, and pull the door back to reveal the winter afternoon outside.

At first, I can't process what I'm looking at. I see Iz. I see the old beater car all decked out like some kind of bedraggled tribute to the glory of Italy, but I can't make sense of any of it all. For a few seconds, I just stand there, motionless on the front porch of Becca's house while my brain tries to take what I'm looking at and turn it into thoughts in my head.

Iz is wearing a white button-down patterned with little black plus signs. I remember the day they found it at a thrift store we visited back in Toronto. They have a black blazer layered on top, and they must be freezing in the chilly air, but even in my state of extreme mental delay, I can appreciate how dashing they look. They're like something out of an eighties teen movie, leaning up against the car like that with one leg crossed in front of the other.

Their face isn't quite as suave. I can see the hesitation there, the trace of panic in the way their eyes are wide and searching. Their jaw is clamped so tight I can see the tension in their features even from here.

Something in me breaks free when our gazes lock, something wild and brave and alive—something that refuses to let me crush it, no matter how many reasons I have to stomp it under my feet.

And that's when it clicks: the car, Italy, the mopeds.

Roman Holiday.

My favourite movie. Iz brought my favourite movie to life—albeit in a very ramshackle, Nova-Scotia-winter-appropriate way.

I can't remember anyone ever doing something quite like this for me.

My hands fly to my mouth, and I can feel the corners of my eyes start to sting. My brain finally catches up with the moment and unleashes a floodgate of feelings: elation, relief, anger, pain, confusion, hope. It's all there, swirling around inside me until I have to let it out with a sob.

"Marina." Iz flies up the path, their face creased with concern, and then stops just at the edge of the porch. Their hands flutter at their sides like they're not sure what to do with them. "Marina."

I can hear the same swirling storm of emotions I'm feeling in the way they say my name. I lower my hands to my sides, my bottom lip trembling, and then I step down off the porch and throw myself into their arms.

There's still so much I need to hear from them. There's so much we need to fix—maybe even too much—but right now, they're here. Right now, we have a chance. I haven't lost them yet.

I cling to them, the two of us taking shaky breaths as they squeeze me tight. I close my eyes and breathe the scent of them in until I feel like I'm ready to speak.

I step back and open my mouth, but they beat me to the punch.

"I was an idiot."

A car rumbles by on the street as we watch each other. After a moment of silence, I dip my chin in a nod.

"You were a dummy dumb dumb."

Their tight-lipped grimace starts to show the trace of a smile, and it gets bigger as the corner of my mouth lifts too.

"A dummy dumb dumb," they repeat, nodding solemnly at the insult we came up with as kids and treated like the most shocking swear word imaginable. "Probably the most of a dumby dumb dumb I've ever been. Marina, I..."

The smile fades, replaced by a twisted pain it takes everything in me not to step forward and do my best to smooth away.

I need to see this pain. I need to hear their regret. I need the truth from them, the truth we've both been dancing around for so long. None of this will matter—the car, the suit, the grand romantic gesture—if they can't give me the truth to hold onto.

"I don't regret kissing you on New Year's Eve." They're quieter now, but their voice is stronger, like the glowing coals in the hottest part of a fire. "It wasn't a mistake. It was the best thing I've ever done. I don't regret holding your hand in my bed a few nights ago. I don't regret every time I've looked at you for longer than friends are supposed look at each other. I don't regret any of it. I just regret how much time it's taken me to accept what you mean to me—what you *really* mean to me, and I regret how much that's hurt you."

It takes everything in me not to reach for them now, but I hold back. I even hold my breath as they keep saying everything I've been waiting to hear.

"You're a goddamn queen, you know that, Marina? You're sweet and kind. You're funny and sassy. You always know how to give as good as you get, and you make me laugh like no one else. You make me feel safe like no one else. You always say the right thing to say to everyone, but especially to me. You're strong. You're a fighter. You overcome everything life throws at you, and you do it all with grace instead of bitterness. I mean...*Mierda*, you are really something else. Sometimes I just stop and stare at you too. All the time, in fact. I always have."

I can't speak, so I just nod. Their eyes search my face,

and I watch them watch me. I know their every detail. I know every little quirk and expression. Even now, when we've come so close to breaking, I'm connected to them in a way I've never been with anyone else.

"Sometimes I feel like we were kids so long ago," they continue, "and sometimes I feel like I'm still a kid now. These past few days, and last night especially, have shown me I have a lot of growing up to do. I have a lot of...of healing to do, and I need to get on with it, or I'm just going to keep hurting people and...and hurting myself. I know you might not be ready to give me another shot, Marina, and I'm not asking you to. Not yet. I'm just asking you not to give up on me. I know I don't really deserve that, but I just can't let you go. I can't."

"Iz." My voice cracks, and I switch to a whisper. "I don't want to let you go either."

They give me the tiniest smile as their eyes start to get shiny. "Good. *Dios*, I really thought you were going to tell me to go to hell. I mean, you still might, but I want to fight for this, Marina. For us."

It's what I've been wanting for so long: a confirmation that I'm not the only one who believes in us.

"I'm so tired of being scared," they tell me, "and I'm tired of pretending I'm not scared. Everything you said last night was true. It was hard to hear, but I needed it. It's like I said: you always know exactly what to say. You know what I need, and today I want to show you I know what you need too. I want to show you I can give it to you."

My heart feels like it's about to explode, but something is still holding me back. I don't know if I can trust this yet. It's almost too good to be true.

"Iz—"

They hold up a hand to stop me. "You don't need to decide or give me anything just yet. You deserve more than just a few words in front of this house after everything I've put you through, so today, I want to give you a chance to put it all on hold and just...be. Here. With me. On a little getaway. A...holiday, if you will."

The typical Iz slyness I know so well slips into their voice, and that alone is almost enough to win me over.

They do know how to be extremely charming.

They step back and make a show of clearing their throat. "Marina Townsend, will you let me take you on your very own Roman holiday?" They swoop their arm out to indicate the car plastered in streamers and pictures of tiny mopeds. "We, uh, couldn't secure a real moped, but this is the next best thing. I mean, maybe a Ferrari would be the next best thing, but I don't think there are any Ferraris in Halifax."

"This is perfect," I say as I step down off the porch. "Where did you get a car?"

"It's uh, kind of a long story. I'll tell you on the road—if you want to go, that is."

I turn from looking at the car to face them. "I do."

They offer me their hand, palm turned up like an old-timey gentleman escorting a lady. We both stay still for a second, and then I clasp my hand over theirs. Warmth floods my whole body the second I do, and somehow, despite everything else I'm feeling, I still get butterflies.

I don't know how someone I've known my whole life manages to give me butterflies, but they do.

"I really do feel like Miss Audrey Hepburn," I mumble as we make our way over to the car.

"Well, Miss Marina Townsend, we may not have the streets of Rome to careen through, but I plan on making this a day fit for a runaway princess."

They keep their hand wrapped around mine as they use their other arm to open the passenger-side door. That's when I notice the tiara perched on top of the headrest and the handwritten note taped to the seat.

Reserved for her Royal Highness.

"Your crown, my fair lady."

Iz grabs the rhinestone-encrusted plastic circlet and fits it around my head as I laugh.

"*My Fair Lady* is a completely different Audrey Hepburn movie."

"Well, then I guess you get to be all the Audrey Hepburns today. Did I tell you this tiara came from Tiffany's? I got it at breakfast."

I full-on snort at that. "Wow, Iz. That might be the worst *Breakfast at Tiffany's* joke I've ever heard."

"I accept that title with pride."

I follow their gesture to get into the car, and they close the door for me as I pull my seatbelt on. I get even more curious about where the car came from as my nose wrinkles at the distinct inhabited-by-a-college-boy-who-doesn't-clean scent lingering in the air.

"Can you confirm this vehicle isn't stolen?" I ask as Iz swings into their seat beside me.

"Do you really want me to confirm that? You don't want a little element of danger on our adventures today?"

"Oh, Iz." I shake my head as I grin at them, and they're smiling right back.

Maybe we still have things to figure out, but this moment is exactly what Iz said it would be: an escape, a getaway, a holiday where we can sit back and be ourselves.

I'm realizing now that we haven't been ourselves this whole trip. We have our rhythm back now, the ease of two people who've spent more hours than they can count by each other's sides. I sink right into that ease like a pool of warm water. I float through the drive around the student neighbourhood while we make stupid jokes and tease each other like we always do. I float through our trip downtown, where Iz points out the car window to show me places they've eaten and drank and danced. I settle back into my seat and listen to their stories, their voice, and all the words I can hear beneath what they're saying.

I'm sorry.

I mean it.

Please let me prove it to you.

Please let me be yours again.

That's the thing: they've always belonged to me, and I've always belonged to them. It's a promise we made with friendship bracelets and little dollar store necklaces that fit together to make the shape of a heart, with pinkie swears and birthday cards inscribed with strings of inside jokes no one else ever understood, with late night phone calls and arms linked as we strode into the first day of high school.

We've been there for each other every step of the way, even when we've struggled. We're weaved into the stories of each other's lives, and this—this thing I want that I'm starting to believe Iz wants too—is just another chapter.

It might even be the best chapter, but we have to take up the pen and write the words.

"So I know it's kind of between meal times, but what do you say to some Davy Jones pizza?"

Their question pulls me out of the trance I've fallen into. I look out my side of the car to see the famous pizza place coming into view as we crest one of the steep hills Halifax is known for. My stomach rumbles at the sight of the pirate ship logo painted on the building's brick wall.

"I could go for some pizza."

"Half barbeque chicken, half pepperoni and cheese?"

Normally I'm not a chicken pizza kind of girl, but it's my go-to order at Davy Jones whenever I'm in town. I swear they sprinkle the stuff with cocaine and fairy dust.

"You know me well, don't you?"

The light-hearted mood between us shifts as they guide the car into a spot along the sidewalk, replaced with something deeper, something breathless and urgent to make itself known.

"I do," they say, turning to face me as they cut the engine. Their voice is barely more than a mumble, but their eyes are flashing with fervour and locked on mine. "I know you so well, Marina. I have you memorized. I meant it when I said I just stop and stare at you sometimes. I don't want to miss a thing."

Yet another part of me I thought was going dark bursts into brilliant light. Ever since I opened the door and saw them leaning against this car, it's like a string of glowing bulbs coming on inside me, one after the other until I'm shining.

"I don't want to miss a thing with you either, Iz."

We sit there for a moment, the sound of our breathing filling the space between us. One of their hands is still clutching the steering wheel, but the other is resting palm-up on the console between us. I stare down at the lines on their palm, a spider web of memories and experiences that have shaped them into who they are.

I hesitate for another moment, and then I fit my palm over theirs and wrap my fingers around their hand, pressing our stories together. Our head lines and heart lines and whatever other lines there are in palmistry touch one another, criss-crossing in infinite trails of possibility.

I hear Iz gasp, and I look up from where I've been staring down at my knuckles. They're watching our hands too, and they squeeze me back when I tighten my grip.

"It just...It feels so...I don't even know what to call it," they stammer. "I mean, even just holding your hand, it's..."

"I know," I say when they don't go on. "I feel it."

They look up at me, their bottom lip trembling, and I'm leaning in before I even realize we've gotten closer. I've dreamt about kissing them for so long—not a quick New Year's Eve peck, but a real kiss, one that lasts long enough for us to lose ourselves and let go.

Some frat boy's car outside a pizza shop is not the place I want that to happen, though, so I pull back and squeeze their hand again before unlatching mine.

"Soon," I mutter. I feel my cheeks going red as another flock of butterflies take off inside my stomach. "Do you want me to come inside with you?"

"I, uh..." They clear their throat and shake their head, the dazed expression I'm sure matches my own slipping off their face. "I mean, what kind of chauffeur would I be if I didn't get your pizza for you?"

I chuckle. "Do chauffeurs do that?"

"This one does. I'll leave the heat on for you too. Five star service."

They spring into action, stepping out of the car and then grabbing a coat I didn't notice off the back seat before heading inside the shop. I lean my tiara-clad head against the back of my seat and close my eyes as I settle in to wait for them.

This is happening.

It's the thought that plays over and over again. I hold onto it like a lifeline as the minutes tick by. Iz is back much sooner than I expect, probably given how unusual it is to be eating a meal at almost three in the afternoon.

"Your pizza, princess."

They deposit the box in the back seat, and the smell of melted cheese and sweet barbeque sauce makes my mouth water.

"It's cute when you call me princess," I say, mostly to

keep myself from grabbing the box and tearing it open right now.

"Oh yeah?"

My cheeks heat up again as we pull away from the sidewalk. "Yeah, I actually like it. It's, uh…"

I stop myself before I can say 'sexy.' I don't know if we're there yet, but having them call me princess like that is making me want to be *there* as fast as possible. With them in that shirt, it's been hard not to imagine steaming up the car windows while I rip the buttons open and pull it off them in the back seat. I know the mood is more on the tender side today, but it doesn't stop me from wanting them.

"I'll keep that in mind," they mutter, the husk in their voice making the muscles of my thighs tighten.

I've got to get a grip. We still have things to say. We still need to establish what we're doing and where we're headed.

Iz seems to be on the same page. They start guiding the car out of the downtown core as they announce they know a good place to talk.

"It's not far," they say. "I think you'll like it. I haven't taken you there before."

We end up crossing back over to the south end of the city, driving down residential streets lined with big trees and tiny houses until we're out of town altogether. The city transitions seamlessly into a coastal park dotted with walking trails and patches of trees.

"This is Point Pleasant Park," they say after we've turned into a small gravel parking lot. "Sometimes I come run here. You know, when it's not covered with snow. I'm not really a snow runner."

"I thought you only ran on the treadmill?"

They've never told me about jogging beside the ocean,

and even in the eternal grey of Halifax winter, this place seems stunning enough to be worth mentioning.

They laugh. "I mean, sometimes I go outside. I didn't even know about this park until Jane took me here last spring to help her look for wildflowers for some craft thing she was doing. Only Jane." They pause to laugh again and then get quieter. "Now it's my thinking place."

"Your thinking place?"

"Yeah, I come here when I've got to work something out, you know? It's been a good place to contemplate the myth of the gender binary and the fact that I'm not a girl." They glance down at the steering wheel. "I haven't ever told anyone I come here by myself. I don't know why. I guess it felt kind of like a secret, and I...I want to share that with you."

I reach over and squeeze their shoulder, brushing my thumb along the fabric of their coat for a second before I let go.

"Thank you. That means a lot."

We get out of the car without saying another word, and Iz carries the pizza as we meander through the park. The cardboard box is steaming in the cold air, and I know we'll need to stop and eat soon if we want hot food, but we keep going for a few more minutes anyway.

The clean smell of winter is laced with the tang of salt from the sea. A few diehard gulls are squawking and circling in the air high above us. We pass a handful of people all bundled up in winter gear. They smile and chuckle at my tiara, but for the most part, we have the place to ourselves. The packed-down snow crunches under our boots, and the constant whoosh of the ocean reminds me to breathe deep and enjoy the moment.

I'm on holiday, after all.

"If we brush the snow off, we could sit there." Iz points

to a picnic table up ahead that faces the ocean. We veer off the path and trudge through the ankle-deep snow to get to it.

"Here, I'll do it. You don't have gloves." I pull my mittens out of my pocket and ignore Iz's protests about being a bad chauffeur as I push enough snow off the table to give us a place to sit.

We take spots side by side right on the tabletop, using one of the benches as a foot rest. Iz props the pizza box on their knees and opens it, unleashing a cloud of steam and the smell of cheesy goodness into the air.

"Okay, I can't wait any longer. I'm digging in." I reach over to extract a slice of barbeque chicken, realizing way too late that we don't have any napkins as sauce and flour from the crust coats my fingers. "This is gonna be messy."

Iz chuckles. "That sounds like a metaphor."

"O' 'ah?" I say around the giant bite I tear off the end of the piece.

They laugh again. "Yeah. I mean..." They gesture between us. "This has definitely been messy, and I know that's my fault."

I speed through chewing while they stare down at the rest of the pizza in their lap.

"It was always going to be messy," I say after I swallow. "I think that's inevitable when you go from friends to...something else, but it probably didn't need to hurt this much."

They nod. "No, it didn't. Hurting you is the worst part of all this. I should have trusted you. I...It's been hard for me to even trust myself, but I should have just told you that instead of fucking it all up because I was scared. I'm still scared, Marina. I'm really scared."

They look at me, and I can see it now: how terrified

they are. They're almost shaking, and still, they're here. They're here getting through this with me.

That means something.

"But I'm done feeling like I'm too much," they continue. "All this time, I've been trying to prove I'm not too much for everybody, but I've been looking in all the wrong places. It's like you said; I've been scared of things going wrong, but I've also been scared of things going right. Sometimes it's easier to trust the bad than the good, but that's..."

They trail off and mutter something in Spanish, their tone sing-songy, like it's something they've said a million times before. I think I recognize the sound of the words, but I can't remember the meaning.

"What does that one mean again?"

"One of my dad's constant refrains," they answer. "It means that's no way to live."

I can hear the regret in their voice, the pain they've been living with for so long as their worst fears play out over and over again with everyone they've dared to care about.

"Iz." If my hands weren't covered in barbeque sauce and clutching a piece of pizza, I'd be reaching for theirs. "You can trust me. It's *me*. I know you've been searching for so long, and maybe...maybe this is it. Maybe this is the answer. You and me."

Their shoulders really do start shaking now. They're still looking down at the cooling pizza.

"I'm here, Iz," I tell them. "I'm in this, but I need to know you are too."

This isn't something we can rush into without laying a foundation. The past few days have made that clearer than ever. We need to be sure we're on the same page if we want more than a shot in the dark.

"I know we'll need time," I continue. "I want time. I want to make sure we do this right, but I need to know we *are* doing it and that neither of us is turning back."

"I'm not turning back from this, Marina." They finally meet my eyes, and I see nothing but truth there. "You have me. I'm in this."

They toss the pizza box onto the table beside them, and before I even realize what's happening, their hands are in my hair and they're pressing their lips to mine.

My eyes close on instinct, and my slice of pizza slips out of my grasp and lands on the ground with a plop. I'd laugh if my heart wasn't about to head straight into cardiac arrest. The realization that Iz is kissing me floods my senses and sends my whole body into overdrive.

Iz is kissing me, and it's more than I ever thought it could be.

For a few seconds, I'm too stunned to kiss them back. I feel them start to pull away, probably worried they've made the wrong move, and the thought of this ending spurs me into action. I grab the front of their shirt and yank them closer.

My lips part, shifting theirs, and the little sigh they make has me kissing them harder than ever as I slip my arms around them under their coat, clutching at their back as their hands lock behind my neck. They tilt my head back, taking charge as we both moan into each other's mouths. They're all I can taste, all I can smell and see and hear as the whole world turns into nothing more than a backdrop for this one incredible kiss.

I let it all out: the joy and the pain. The waiting and wanting. The future and the past. We kiss for so long I can't tell the difference between seconds and minutes anymore, but it's still not enough. I will never get enough of this.

Kissing Iz feels like coming home.

When we're finally breathless enough that we need to break apart, I let them pull their lips from mine but still keep my arms twined around their body. We're both panting, and their eyes are just glittering slits as they watch me. I can feel the need radiating off them, and it's just as strong as my own.

There's no awkwardness, no hesitation. I expected more of a transition period after almost two decades of friendship, but there's nothing like that in this moment. Everything about this feels right, like we've been headed here our whole lives.

"Wow," they finally say, still panting.

"Wow," I echo.

We both let out a breathless laugh and shift so there's a bit of space between us.

"I mean...wow," they repeat. "That was...*wow*."

"Yeah. You know it's a good kiss when it makes me drop my Davy Jones pizza."

"Oh, *mierda*!" They glance at the sacrificed slice laying face-down in the snow. "I totally forgot you were eating that."

"Well, you'll remember it when you find all the barbeque sauce on your shirt. I really hope that washes out. We need to save this shirt for posterity."

We move another few inches apart so we can both take in the damage to the front of Iz's button-down. A few clumps of sauce mark the spot where I grabbed them.

"Worth it," they say with a grin.

"Yeah." I shift closer. "So worth it."

Heat sparks to life low in my stomach as we both start to lean in again, but then Iz grabs my shoulders to hold me in place.

"Okay, wait. Before we do that again and I completely

lose my mind in the best way possible, there's something this moment deserves."

"What's that?" I ask, my brain already kiss-drunk again.

"A pizza toast!"

"Oh my god." I roll my eyes and pretend to be annoyed. "That's what you interrupted this for?"

"Pizza toasts are good luck!" They grab two slices and thrust one into my hands before holding theirs up in the air. "To us!"

I take the sight of them in, hair all dishevelled from the kiss with sauce streaking their shirt and their face lit up like a sunrise.

I'd take a picture, but I already know I'll never forget a single detail of how they look right now.

"To us," I repeat.

We slam our slices together, and I don't give them a chance to take a bite. I fling both pieces to the ground and then pull Iz to me, capturing their mouth in another kiss that seems to last forever and not long enough all at once.

I don't mind. I know there's plenty more where that came from.

13

Iz

"How the hell did I get so lucky?"

I set the framed cross stitch down on my bedside table as gently as I can before lunging for Marina on my bed. I throw my arms around her neck and settle my chin on her shoulder, her body warming mine as she grabs me around the waist to hug me back.

"I can't believe you made me a custom cross stitch for my birthday. It's officially my new favourite thing ever."

She chuckles next to my ear. "What about your Jordans?"

"Hmm." I pretend to think. "*One* of my favourite things ever."

She starts to pull away, making a show out of being offended, but I refuse to let her go. She gives in and groans after a moment, leaning back into the hug.

We stayed out longer than I thought we would today. After managing to eat the rest of our pizza without dropping it on the ground, we took a walk around the park that lasted over an hour. We talked about big things like trust and courage, and small things like sunbeams glinting on the ocean and how the seagulls freaked us both out with how fast they went after the pizza.

We laughed and sighed and even teared up a few times, and we walked out of the park holding hands.

We went for another drive around the city after that, all the way up to the north end and then across to Dartmouth and back again. By then we were hungry for dinner, so we grabbed donairs and had bubble tea for dessert. We walked around the harbor sipping up sugary milk and tapioca pearls, reminiscing about our favourite bubble tea place back in Toronto.

Now we're here, in my bedroom, with my body pressed to hers and my mind steadier than it's been in weeks.

We sit like that for a moment, just breathing. I can smell the jasmine in her hair and the sweet scent of her neck. All I'd have to do is tilt my head an inch to kiss her there.

A thrill runs through me, starting low in my stomach and almost growing strong enough to make me shiver. Just thinking about kissing her again makes me so nervous I'm in danger of sweating harder than I do at lacrosse practice, but as much as she's the cause of the nerves, she's also the thing that calms them. When I look at her—really look at her, until everything else fades—there's no fear in those nerves. There's only excitement.

I'm excited for what comes next in our lives, because whatever it is, it's going to be fucking awesome.

I'm in love with my best friend.

I repeat the words to myself as I press my lips to the soft skin just below her ear.

That thought used to keep me up at night, heart racing and dread turning my stomach over, but now all I want to do is laugh at past Iz for freaking out over being one of the luckiest damn people in the world.

"Wow," Marina whispers when I pull my mouth away after a second.

"Was that okay?"

"Yeah, I just...This all feels even better than I imagined. I thought it might be a little weird at first, and it does feel very new, but it also just...fits. We just fit."

I drop my arms from around her and lean back so I can take the sight of her in. She's beaming, glowing with the same feeling that's making my chest swell.

"Yeah. We do."

She takes my hands in hers, and I force a chuckle as another thrill shoots through me like a whole pack firecrackers going off at once.

"I am a little nervous," I tell her, "but you make me feel safe. I used to feel like I was stuck walking on a tightrope, just trying to make it through this without falling, but now..."

I trail off and stare down at my hands, biting back what I was about to say. I'm not going to get *that* cheesy.

"But now?" Marina prompts.

I wouldn't be surprised if she's already guessed the end of my sentence. That may be a tricky part of dating my best friend: she has a lifetime of experience in reading my mind.

I shrug, but she squeezes my hands and then shakes them when I don't go on. I give in and start laughing when she begins swooping our hands in big dramatic circles while chanting for me to tell her.

"Okay, okay. You'll never let me live this down, but...I was gonna say, it's not like I'm stuck on a tightrope anymore. It's like...It's like I'm flying."

She stays quiet, her smile fading.

"Too much?" I ask.

I wince, bracing for her to shut me down, but all she does is shake her head.

"Marina?" I say after another few seconds of silence. "What's up?"

"I just—" She cuts herself off and presses her lips into a tight line, shaking her head again.

"You what? Don't leave me hanging here, Marina." I start copying her dramatic hand circles from earlier, making us both sway as I chant. "Tell me. Tell me. Tell me."

She snorts and then lets out a full-on guffaw.

"You goon," she gasps before breaking into a laugh attack that leaves her fighting for air. "I was trying not to laugh because it's—it's s-so sweet and it means so much, and I d-didn't want to-to—"

"Oh my god, Marina." I make a big deal out of pretending to be insulted, dropping one of her hands to press my own to my forehead. "You're laughing at my cheesy flying metaphor, aren't you? This is why I didn't want to tell you. You are so cruel to me."

I drop her other hand and let myself tip back onto the mattress.

"I shared my poetry with you, and you mocked me," I moan as I drag my hands down my face and start thrashing on the blankets. "I will never recover."

"Oh my god, you drama queen."

She groans and leans over me to pry my hands away from my face and pin them above my head.

"You know it was a *little* cheesy," she says, the tips of her hair tickling my cheek.

Honestly, I don't even remember what we're talking about. My heart is beating so hard I can feel it drumming in my ears and temples. I can feel her warm breath on my face, and all I can think about is the way she tasted in the park this afternoon.

"But it was also so incredibly sweet," she continues, "and beautiful and, yes, poetic. It was exactly what I needed to hear."

There's an edge to her voice, like she's got something up her sleeve. I shift a little on the bed and have to squeeze my thighs together when the feeling of her hands keeping me firmly in place makes me twitch with how bad I want her.

"But?" I prompt.

"But I need to make sure you're not pulling your little charmer act on me." She leans in even closer, and my breath catches in my throat. "You can be very charming, Iz, with your dapper button-downs and your flashy Jordans and your poetic metaphors."

"No charmer act here." I shake my head, my voice hoarse. "I guess I'm just a natural."

I can see her fighting not to laugh again, but to her credit, she keeps up the seduction act despite me being a complete dork.

"I want you to kiss me again, Iz." She's even closer now, so close I can already feel the teasing ghost of her lips on mine as I close my eyes. "I want you to...show me what flying feels like."

I crack my eyes back open, and we both lose it, howling with laughter and rolling apart so we can clutch our stomachs and gasp for air only to start laughing again.

"Touche, touché," I wheeze when I can finally talk again. "I'm really getting burned here, aren't I?"

"I swear I didn't plan on saying that," Marina says through the last of her giggling. It's very cute when she giggles. "The opportunity just presented itself."

I watch her swipe at the corners of her eyes and then

run a hand through her hair. She's sitting up on the bed now, and I push myself upright beside her. Her freckles look so soft and sweet in the lamplight, and for a second, I stop to appreciate just how goddamn stunning she is.

"Marina."

She turns to me, and I don't wait another second. I frame her face with my hands and kiss her like I'll never get to kiss her again.

She gasps and parts her lips for me, and I slip my tongue inside her mouth for the first time. We both moan, clutching at each other, touching and tasting and memorizing the way it feels to be this close.

I don't ever want to forget. I don't ever want to give myself time to forget. I want to keep kissing her for the rest of my life.

We're chest to chest with me practically in her lap when I tip her backwards and straddle her, neither of us breaking the kiss for a second as she grabs my hips and pulls me closer. I'm fully on top of her now, her body arching to meet mine, and I can't remember ever wanting someone even half this much before.

It's more than that; I *need* her. I need her in more ways than I could ever count, and somehow, by whatever miracle I've been lucky enough to get caught up in, she seems to need me too.

It's enough to have my eyes start stinging again. This is so much. It's perfect in every way, but it might be too much for tonight.

I bury my face in her neck instead of kissing her more, breathing deep as her hands slide up from my hips to start rubbing my back.

"Iz," she whispers after a moment, "I, um, I really want you, but I think maybe we should slow down?"

"Yeah," I whisper back. "Slow would be good. I want to make sure we're ready."

I roll onto my side next to her, and she catches one of my hands to twine her fingers with mine. We lay beside each other in the dark, and even though we don't say it out loud, I can feel the weight of tomorrow sinking in.

Tomorrow: the day she leaves.

"You know, just yesterday I was looking into moving my flight up, and now I wish I could push it back," she says, making it clear we're both riding the same somber thought train.

I wince at the thought of what she must have been going through yesterday, stuck in this city when all she probably wanted was to go home.

"I'm so sorry. I'm sorry it hurt that much," I murmur as I squeeze her hand. "It's not ever going to hurt that much again."

She tilts her head, her eyes finding mine.

"I know." She nods. "Doesn't make leaving easier, though. It's like we just got this thing, and now we've already got to put it to the test."

"Well, to use another poetic metaphor: if this is a test, then we'll ace it. I know we will." I prop my head on my hand so I can see her better. "I'm in this, Marina."

She scoots over, bringing her face just an inch from mine. "Me too."

She's the one who leans in this time. The kiss is soft and sweet, both of us taking our time in a way we haven't yet, but all it takes is one sweep of her tongue along my bottom lip to have me fisting my hand in her hair.

"Goddamn," I hiss when she pulls away.

Her eyes have gone all hazy, and there's a lopsided smile on her face. "You make going slow very difficult."

"I could say the same about you."

She sighs and flops onto her back again, stretching her hands above her head and arching her back in a way that does not make it easy to refrain from saying 'fuck it all' and jumping her.

"Maybe we could watch a show or something. First I gotta shower. I just remembered I haven't showered today."

"Are you trying to drive me crazy?" I demand. "I find it hard to believe you're innocently stretching and talking about being in my shower."

She sits up and throws me a coy look over her shoulder. "Guess I'm a natural."

She stands up and grabs a few things from her suitcase before flouncing off to the bathroom without another word. I tip onto my back again and groan as soon as she's gone. Marina was always very good at platonically teasing me. Sexual teasing from her is going to destroy me.

But I love it.

I listen to the shower come on down the hall. I can hear the muffled sound of my housemates having a movie night downstairs. They showed an uncharacteristic amount of restraint when Marina and I walked in earlier. All we got were a few raised eyebrows and fake-casual greetings of 'Oh hey, guys.'

I guess they were waiting for me to take the lead on dropping the news, but I'm not sure I'm ready to share what's happened between us just yet.

I settle my hands behind my head and let flashes of the day play out on the backs of my eyelids as I wait for Marina: her face when I showed up with the car, the way she looked at me the second before I kissed her for the first time, the grin on her face as she clinked her bubble tea cup with mine.

She looked familiar and new all at once, like walking

into your bedroom at a time you usually aren't home and seeing the sun glint on the edge of your mirror, painting the walls with little rainbows you've never been there to notice before.

She'd tease the shit out of me about that one, but it's true.

I don't want to miss more of those moments. I want to be there with her every day, and maybe that's not possible now, but at the very least, I don't want to face tomorrow on my own.

We still have so much to share.

I want to let us have that.

I jump to my feet and dart over to her suitcase. I start digging around through all the compartments, searching for the paper I know must be here. Marina is the kind of person who always prints her boarding pass even if she has it on her phone.

I find the ticket tucked into the front flap of the bag and bring it over to my desk. It only takes a few minutes of searching around on my laptop before I find a shamefully overpriced last-minute ticket for the same flight.

I open up a second tab to look at my bank account and wince. Combined with the return trip I'll need to figure out and book later, this will wipe out a huge chunk of my summer job savings.

I take a deep breath and let the surge of adrenaline building inside me overflow.

I'm doing this.

"Guess I'm eating instant noodles until May," I mutter as I click back to the airline's site and start typing in my information.

I've just gotten the confirmation email when Marina comes back in the room, already in her pajamas with her damp hair hanging loose over her shoulders.

"Damn," I say, freezing with my fingers hovering over the keyboard. "Now that I'm allowed to stare at you without it being weird, I really can't stop."

She smiles and drops her eyes to the floor, a little shy despite her Miss Super Cocky routine earlier.

"Such a charmer," she mutters. "So, you finding us something to watch on Netflix?"

I glance back at my inbox. "Um, no, actually."

She looks over her shoulder from where she's crouched down to put her clothes in her bag. "Got distracted?"

"I...kind of."

It hits me then: I really just bought a ticket to Kingston tomorrow. I bought a plane ticket after about two minutes of contemplation, and I didn't even check with Marina.

"So..." I stand up and brush my palms down the front of my thighs. "I might have done something impulsive."

She straightens up and raises her eyebrows. "Oh?"

"Yeah. So. I was thinking about what you said, and as much as I believe there's nothing that could stop me from fighting for this, it really does suck to have to start fighting for it right away. We deserve a few days of appreciating just how crazily awesome this is."

The guarded curiosity doesn't leave her face, but the corner of her mouth lifts. "It *is* crazily awesome."

"Right. I want you to be sure of what this means to me and how serious I am. I don't want you to have to doubt. It's new and exciting and still kind of scary, but it's what I want, so..." I look back at my computer and point at the screen. "I'm coming with you tomorrow."

"*What?*"

She runs over to check the email herself, her eyes darting around the screen as they get wider and wider.

"Oh my god, Iz." She takes a step back from the desk. "You did that. You're coming with me. You..." She turns to look at me, her eyes getting glassy as she drops her voice to a whisper. "You really want this."

I move to stand right in front of her. "I do, Marina."

She throws her arms around my neck, and I slide mine around her waist. She hums and starts to sway, and we both start laughing and twisting in place until we're full-on dancing with each other.

"You're coming with me!" she shouts.

"I'm coming with you!" I shout back.

She lets out an excited shriek, and the two of us start jumping up and down. I'm about to pull her into a kiss again when a knock at my door interrupts us.

"What is this ruckus about?" Jane's voice demands. I can hear how thrilled she is even through the door.

"Are you decent?" Hope adds. "We're coming in!"

Marina and I are still frozen mid-celebration when Jane, Hope, and Paulina come charging into the room.

"Oh my god, they're in LOVE!" Paulina screams when she sees our joined hands. "It worked!"

"Yeah, it—"

I don't have time to finish my sentence before she's lunging for me, tackling me with all six foot one of her height and sending me toppling forward against Marina. Hope and Jane add themselves to the pile-up a minute later, the three of them squeezing us all into a group hug that's definitely constricting my lungs.

The asphyxiation is worth it. As they scooch in even closer and ply us with rapid-fire questions asked way too fast for me to actually give them any answers, I feel the last of the day's tension slipping away.

I have my friends. I have Marina. I have a plane ticket booked for tomorrow, and everything is going to be okay.

"It was that pizza toast!" Hope shouts over everyone

else's clamouring voices. "I knew that pizza toast I made was gonna get you two together. It's good luck!"

"It's gross," Marina says from where she's pressed up against me, laughing at my crazy friends. "But yeah, I guess it worked."

"To Marina and Iz!" Jane crows. "Hip, hip, hooray!"

And then these weirdos I call my best friends all break apart and start doing a medieval-style round of 'hip, hip, hoorays' like the dorks they are. They make a circle around me and Marina, linking arms and bringing all their joined hands in towards us with every cheer.

"So, uh, this is fun," I say, leaning in to bring my mouth close to Marina's ear.

"This is perfect." Her hands find mine. "To us."

I lift our hands up right in time for the final 'hooray,' throwing my head back and closing my eyes just long enough to commit this moment to memory forever.

This is our beginning.

"To us."

-Katia

About the Author

Katia Rose is not much of a Pina Colada person, but she does like getting caught in the rain. She loves to write romances that make her readers laugh, cry, and swoon (preferably in that order). She's rarely found without a cup of tea nearby, and she's more than a little obsessed with tiny plants. Katia is proudly bisexual and has a passion for writing about love in all its forms.

www.katiarose.com

Club Katia

Club Katia is a community that comes together to celebrate the awesomeness of romance novels and the people who read them. Joining also scores you some freebies to read!

Membership includes special updates, sneak peeks, access to Club Katia Exclusives (a collection of content available especially to members) and the opportunity to interact with fellow members in the Club Katia Facebook Group.

Joining is super easy and the club would love to have you! Visit www.katiarose.com/club-katia to get in on the good stuff.

Also by Katia Rose

The Barflies Series

A series of dramadies centred on the lives and loves of the staff
at a Montreal dive bar. Each novel can be read as a standalone.

The Bar Next Door

Glass Half Full

One For the Road

When the Lights Come On

The Sherbrooke Station Quartet

A series of steamy rock star dramadies that follow the rise of an
alternative rock band in Montreal. All four volumes can be read
as standalones.

Your Rhythm

Your Echo

Your Sound

Your Chorus

Standalone Novels

Catch and Cradle

The UNS Women's lacrosse team has a pact: no dating your
teammates. Hope was fine with that pact. Then she met Becca.
A laugh-out-loud college sports rom-com.

Thigh Highs

Modelling lingerie for her arch-nemesis was not on Christina's to-do list. Then again, nether was he. An enemies-to-lovers romantic comedy.

Latte Girl

Hot coffee is a regular fixture in Hailey Warren's life. Hot guys? Not so much. A caffeine-fuelled romantic comedy.

Up Next
CATCH AND CRADLE

Thou shalt not date thine teammates.

The UNS Women's Lacrosse team doesn't have an official policy against inter-teammate relationships, but those words might as well be carved into stone tablets in the middle of the field. After witnessing way too much drama in the past, Captain Becca Moore is intent on keeping her players' love lives out of the locker room.

Becca has no time or tolerance for any distractions from the game. Unfortunately, that's exactly what Hope Hastings has been since the day she showed up for tryouts: one walking, talking, charismatically dorky and way-too-kissable distraction.

Hope knew she was headed straight to the danger zone from the moment she saw Becca's flame-red hair and surly captain smirk. She's spent the past two years writing off her attraction as a harmless crush, but starting a new semester fresh out of an awful relationship makes Hope realize just how far from harmless the heat between her and Becca really is.

The friendships of a tight-knit team and their shot at the title are all lying on the line, but as Hope and Becca get closer to bending rules they've sworn never to break, they realize they've put their hearts on that line too. Losing has never been an option, but winning might cost more than they're willing to pay.

***Catch and Cradle* is a New Adult F/F romance from Katia Rose that's filled with all the hilarity and heartache of finding your way through college while discovering love, friendship, and what it means to be yourself.**

Read on for a free excerpt!

1

Hope

There's a gnome wearing a thong and a pair of lacrosse goggles in our front window.

I pause in the middle of the sidewalk, the clatter of my suitcase wheels on the pavement coming to an abrupt stop. My Uber driver takes off up the darkening street, and I turn to watch the car round the corner before looking back at the gnome.

His name is CJ Junior, and my whole face splits into a grin as I raise two fingers to give him a salute.

"It's good to be back," I mutter as I charge through the little patch of dirt and struggling weeds we call a yard. My suitcase bumps against the wooden stoop as I haul it along behind me up to the front door.

Even if there weren't a gnome dressed in my old lacrosse goggles and a cherry-red thong donated by one of my roommates staring out the window, it wouldn't take a stranger long to realize a bunch of UNS athletes live here. The butter-yellow row house is so narrow it looks like it was squeezed onto the street as an afterthought, but that hasn't stopped us from pimping it out. Besides CJ Junior, the front window is decorated with strings of pink mini lights. We've been told the sultry pink glow makes it look like we're running a gnome brothel, but I kind of like the effect.

The upstairs window is covered with the huge University of Nova Scotia banner Iz, one of my three roommates, uses as a curtain. Our miniscule excuse for a yard has some UNS pinwheels we may or may not have stolen from an orientation event stuck in the ground amidst all the terra cotta pots that house Paulina's perpetually failed attempts to grow an herb garden.

Under my feet is the custom welcome mat Jane had printed when we first moved into the house in our second year. The black block letters spell out 'Welcome to the Babe Cave.'

I remember when we rolled the mat out one August night just like this. The four of us sat on the stoop for hours drinking spiked lemonade in the heat, smacking mosquitoes off our arms and breathing in the faint trace of salty ocean you can usually catch on the breeze in Halifax. I don't know if it's true, but I always think I can smell the ocean more at night.

I fill my lungs up with briny air and take a minute to let the day roll off me: the goodbye with my parents, the rush and roar of the airport, the flight in a tiny tin can of a plane. I let it all go.

One thing at a time. First thing's first.

Phrases like that have kept me on track for years: little reminders that there's always a next step, and I always have what it takes to get there.

I reach for the tarnished brass doorknob, but before I can grab it, the door is jerked back so hard it slams against the wall inside.

"HOPE IS HERE!"

Jane and Paulina scream and squeal as they throw their arms around me, and I'm screaming and squealing too. The three of us start jumping up and down with our arms woven around each other like a complicated Celtic friendship knot and come dangerously close to falling off the stoop.

"You *guysssss!*" Paulina gushes from above me and Jane. She's six foot one, so she's pretty much always above us. The ends of her long blonde hair are currently in danger of suffocating me. "I'm *sooooo* happy!"

She folds herself nearly in half to lay her head on top of mine and nuzzles into me. We stand there swaying and laughing for long enough one of my arms starts to go numb, but I don't care. We've all been in and out of the house throughout the summer, but this is our first real reunion. Lacrosse training camp starts tomorrow, and the fall semester starts a week after that.

The Babe Cave is officially back in business.

"Hey, wait!" I say, twisting my head so I'm not speaking into Jane's shoulder. My glasses have been knocked out of place, but I can't extract my hand to fix them. "Where's Iz?"

Our fourth roommate normally would have joined the pile by now.

"They're picking up dinner," Jane answers.

"You guys didn't eat yet? It's almost eight!"

Paulina lifts her head off me. "Oh, we had dinner. This is second dinner. We thought you'd be hungry after your flight. Iz is getting pizza!"

My mom made a giant early dinner before I left, but my mouth still waters at the thought of pizza.

"From Davy Jones?" I ask.

I can't really see Jane's face, but I feel her nodding. "Of course."

"Fuck yeah! I've been craving Davy Jones pizza all summer. You guys are the best. You know that?"

"Oh, we know."

I start strategizing about how we're going to get out of this group hug without landing in the yard when Paulina lets out a wail.

"NOOO! My basil!"

She tries to pull away to grieve over what must be a freshly dead herb, but we're all so tangled up that Jane and I get tugged along with her. I stumble off the edge of the stoop, fighting to keep my balance. Jane thuds into my back, which sends me careening forward like a domino to thump against Paulina. She sprawls forward and catches herself against the edge of the house before dropping to her knees to grab one of the plant pots and hoist it in the air.

"WHY CRUEL WORLD?" she shouts loud enough for her voice to echo in the street.

I turn to Jane after we've both righted ourselves from nearly falling on our faces. We have an entire silent conversation as we both bite our lips to keep from laughing at Paulina. We're all close in the Babe Cave, but Jane and I have had our own secret best friend language since pretty much the moment we met.

After making the wordless decision to leave Paulina to her mourning—since she's probably going to be out here for at least half an hour poking around at her plants—I pat her on the shoulder and announce that I'm going to put my stuff in my room.

"You all right?" Jane asks as we kick off our shoes in the narrow entranceway. Everything about the house is narrow. "You must be right tired."

Her words are tinged with a slight Nova Scotian accent that makes her sound like an old fisherman's wife trapped in the body of a twenty year-old university student. Paulina, Iz, and I are all from Ontario, and we call Jane our 'local flavour.' Her accent comes out even stronger when she's angry, and she has a way of putting her hands on her hips and tapping her foot like anyone who pisses her off is a misbehaving husband coming home late from the pub.

At the moment, it's just a subtle lilt. She insists on taking the tote bag I have perched on top of my suitcase so I can start hauling my stuff up the creaky stairs. I can smell something sugary drifting up from the ground floor even when I reach the top of the staircase.

"What's the candle flavor of the day?" I ask Jane as she trudges up behind me.

Her obsession with scented candles is legendary. She uses the converted office downstairs as a bedroom, and she's always got some weird smell filling up the house. I actually like the one she's using today.

"Caramel apple. Isn't it heavenly?" She takes a deep breath and raises her eyes to the ceiling as her mouth goes slack with bliss.

"Okay, okay. Don't have a candlegasm."

I roll my suitcase down the creaky floorboards of the hall. There isn't much in this house that doesn't creak. The door to my room is open, and so are my curtains. Dusk has almost turned to night now, but the annoying streetlight that filters through the leaves of a tree in our backyard casts everything in a greenish-yellow glow.

My bed is stripped, and the top of my desk is clearer than it's ever been during a semester, but other than that, the room looks like I could have woken up here instead of halfway across the country. Lacrosse gear is tucked on shelves and hooks as functional decor. A big UNS flag covers one of my closet doors, and there's a Pride flag tacked to the other. A framed photo of my first lacrosse team back in my hometown hangs over my desk, and the wall behind my headboard is covered by a huge art print of chickadees sitting on a branch. The drawing matches the sleeve tattoo on my left upper arm. There's a stained glass chickadee hanging in the window too, lit up from behind by the streetlamp.

I click the overhead light on and wheel my suitcase inside. I set it down under the display of Polaroid photos I made by clipping them to strings with mini clothespins. Jane comes in behind me, and we stare at the photos together.

"Look at what little babies we were!" I point at a shot of her with her arms around my neck in the campus sports bar, the two of us wearing jerseys and clearly wasted. It was taken after lacrosse season ended in our freshman year.

"Oh my god, my cheeks are right chubby in that. Freshman fifteen much?"

"Jane!" I punch her in the arm. "You are a sexy moth-erfucker, and you know it."

Jane is one of the most down to earth, breezily confi-dent people I know, but I also know being a curvy athlete has been hard for her.

She stares at the photo for another second and then nods. "Yes. Yes I am. Especially in this one! Oooh, and look at you! This was just after you got your hair dyed."

She points at another photo, this one taken at the start of the summer just after I'd gotten back from a trip to Montreal. I finished exams earlier than most people, so I went to visit my brother and ended up getting the teal ombre of my dreams from his hairstylist girlfriend. In the picture, Jane and I are both wearing smokey eye makeup we tried and failed to copy from a YouTube tutorial. We're not really a makeup household, but we wanted to get all sexy to celebrate the end of term.

Jane steps closer to squint at another photo. "And aww look! It's all of us and—oh."

I can't stop myself from flinching when I spot the reason for the *oh*.

I thought I got rid of all my photos of him. I want to grab the Polaroid and possibly rip it into a million tiny pieces, but my whole body has gone rigid. I can't even turn around to hide the stupid stinging in my eyes from Jane.

"Oh, Hope!" Her face creases when she looks at me. "Come here. Let me give you a Jane hug."

She throws her arms around me and squeezes hard enough to push the air out of my lungs. I flap my hands against her sides since she isn't letting me move enough to pat her on the back.

"Thanks, Jane." I'm grateful my voice isn't shaking. "I'm fine. He's just a fucking asshole."

She pulls back to hold me at arm's length and nods with a fierce gleam in her eyes. "Yeah, that's right. That fucking turd."

I burst out laughing. "Turd is most certainly the word."

She drops my arms, and I unclip the photo before making a dramatic show of ripping it up while she cheers me on. I drop the pieces in the empty trash can by my desk.

"Now that is a good note to start the term on," she says as she applauds. "We should drink to that."

"That would be cutting it close. Dry season starts tomorrow, and isn't training camp at eight?" I wag my eyebrows. "Aren't you supposed to be the responsible one?"

She puts her hands on her hips. "I'll be responsible tomorrow. Tonight I'm busting out the whiskey."

I whoop and lead the way out of the room. I need the

few seconds it will take to get downstairs to pull myself together.

I spent the summer at home doing everything I could to stop the words he said—*screamed*—from playing on a loop in my head, but all it's taken is one stupid Polaroid to hear them again.

You are crazy and selfish and you wasted a year and a half of my life.

I can still remember how the whole room got quiet, like they'd been waiting for a cue. Drake went on singing about one dance over the sound system, but the entire party stopped.

I wish the worst part was that he'd ruined a perfectly good Drake song for me. I wish he'd done something cliché and stupid like break up with me because I'm bi or because he felt weird dating a girl with more muscles than him.

It's hard to write him off as a complete asshole when a lot of what he said made sense.

A few deep breaths of caramel apple help calm me down enough to push the memories away for now. I roll my shoulders back and lift my chin after I've made it off the last stair, the way my mom taught me to do when I feel bad about myself. Jane has only just caught up behind me when the front door swings open and Iz walks in carrying a stack of pizza boxes while Paulina trails in behind them clutching her basil pot.

"SOAP OF HOPE!" Iz shouts. They zoom past me to dump the boxes off in the living room before zooming right back to pull me into a back-slapping hug.

"Iz, that is such a weird nickname." I laugh as I pull them closer.

"No, it's unique and cool," they correct me. "Just like me."

They pull back to smile at me, and I have to agree:

they are very unique and cool. Their shaved head is topped by a backwards UNS baseball cap, and they've paired raggedy cargo shorts and a green plaid shirt over an expensive-looking pair of high-top basketball shoes.

Iz exists almost exclusively in five dollar finds from the thrift store, but their compulsive splurging on designer Jordans is a force to be reckoned with.

When they came out as non-binary last year, Jane, Paulina, and I all chipped in to buy them a pair in the non-binary pride colours to celebrate. For a few weeks after, it was hard to convince them to even take the shoes off for lacrosse practice.

"Jumping Jesus, you think you got enough pizza, Iz?" Jane is shifting through the boxes in the living room. There *is* a lot of pizza there, even for four college athletes.

"It's Davy Jones!" Iz protests. "I had to get all the good flavours."

"I'm hungry enough to eat half of these." I head over to plop down on the squishy royal blue sofa next to Paulina, who's picking the few remaining leaves off the withered basil plant she has sitting in her lap and scattering them on one of the pizzas.

"I killed this plant, but at least I can honor it in death," she says in a forlorn voice without looking up.

The rest of us all exchange looks and struggle to hold back our laughter. I pat Paulina on the shoulder, but I don't trust myself enough to attempt to say something encouraging.

"Okay, wait, before you dig into the pizza, we need to raise a toast!" Jane disappears into the kitchen for a moment, and after some clanking of glasses and banging of cupboards, she comes back with a bottle of whiskey and four shot glasses.

"*Por dios!*" Iz slaps their thighs. "Hitting the hard stuff already. Can this be our sweet Jane?"

"One shot isn't going to hurt us, and we've got a whole dry season to get through starting tomorrow." She sets the glasses down on the giant coffee table that serves as the Babe Cave's unofficial command station and starts pouring.

Iz gets up to turn the sound system on, and Paulina continues covering our pizza in half-dead basil leaves. I look around at the three of them, and for the second time tonight, heat pricks the corners of my eyes.

This is it. This is our third year. The first semester will fly by like it always does, and before we know it, we'll be in our fourth and final year and on our way out the door. Sometimes it feels like I just went through orientation yesterday, and sometimes it feels like UNS has been my whole life, but it never feels like enough.

I always want more of these moments.

"Hey, you guys." Everyone turns to look at me, and I swallow to keep my voice from shaking. "We should make this a year to remember, yeah? I want...I want it to be special. You guys have been the best two years of my life, and I don't...I don't want to waste...I..."

Paulina squeezes my shoulder, and Jane looks at me like she's close to tears too. I push my glasses up and swipe at my eyes, pissed I can't seem to get myself under control tonight.

"I guess what I'm saying is that we don't have all that much of this left." I gesture around the room filled with UNS memorabilia, photos of us, and a mix of cheap IKEA furniture and second-hand finds. "We should make it count."

I hear Paulina sniff, and a moment of silence passes

before Iz grabs one of the shot glasses and hoists it in the air.

"NO RAGRETS!" they shout, quoting a meme we have stuck to our fridge.

"NO RAGRETS!" we all roar like only sports-obsessed jocks can.

I grab a shot glass for myself and tip the burning liquid into my mouth.

2

Hope

Turns out Jane was right; one shot didn't hurt us, but I'm starting to think the fourth might be doing some damage.

I'm lying on my stomach on the couch, watching Iz and Paulina dance around in the pink glow of our string lights while Jane sits beside me with my feet in her lap. She's scarfing down what has to be her millionth piece of pizza.

Piece of pizza is such a funny phrase.

"Piecccce a' pizza!" I slur before laughing to myself.

"Whas' at?" Jane says around a mouthful of pepperoni and cheese.

"I said piecccccce a' piiiizza!"

A full-on laugh attack takes over, and Jane calls me crazy before slapping me on the ass.

"Owww!" I yelp, but it only makes me laugh even more. I wait for the hysterics to stop and then realize the room is spinning. "Wow, I am officially drunk."

"No shit." Jane slaps my butt again. "Look at the whiskey."

I work very hard to get my eyes to focus on the whiskey bottle on the table in front of me. "Oh. No whiskey."

After the first toast, everybody started wanting to make toasts of their own, and now I can't feel my toes.

"Are you drunk?" I ask Jane.

"Mhmmm." She grunts as she finishes off her final bite of pizza crust. "I'm not being very responsible. CJ is gonna be pisssssssed."

I laugh as I imagine CJ—AKA Coach Jamal, AKA our gnome CJ Junior's namesake—yelling at our sorry hungover asses tomorrow. It really isn't funny; I should be trying to hydrate and get to bed immediately to avoid his wrath, but the whiskey has turned the whole world slow and sticky.

"Not to mention Becca," Jane adds. "She'll probably beat us all with her stick in the locker room before Coach can even get to us."

Jane laughs to herself, but I don't join in. I forgot I'd be seeing Becca tomorrow.

How the fuck did I forget about Becca?

"Need more whiskey," I mumble as I push myself up to a seat.

I grab the bottle even though it's empty and hold it upside down to wait for the final dregs clinging to the glass to trickle into my mouth. I spent the entire day so focused on handling post-breakup feelings about Ethan that I forgot all about handling Becca feelings.

Becca Moore is a force to be reckoned with, both on the lacrosse field and in my thoughts and dreams. This will be her second year as team captain.

Her second year of ordering us around on the field.

Her second year of shouting commands in that smokey, throaty voice of hers.

Her second year of standing on the sidelines to oversee

our warm up drills with her arms crossed in that specific way that makes her tits look inhumanly perfect.

How one person got blessed with thick, flaming red hair, adorable freckles, the kind of brown eyes guys with guitars write songs about, and the C-cups of the century is beyond me.

I'd probably be jealous if I wasn't so obsessed with thinking about kissing her.

Among other things.

I set the whiskey bottle down and wait for the alcohol to take the edge off my pounding heartbeat.

That's all Becca is: a little obsession. A fun, forbidden fantasy.

Emphasis on the forbidden. Our team takes its unofficial 'no banging your teammates' policy more seriously than some of the codified rules of the sport. The team has always been super queer-friendly, but from tryouts onwards, not dating each other is something of a social contract. Apparently there was some drama in the past, and now that we're the first maritime university to play for the Eastern Canada Lacrosse League, keeping our love lives out of the locker room is essential.

That's still never stopped me from imagining pushing Becca up against a wall in the locker room.

"Yo, Hastings!" Iz snaps me out of my trance and motions for me to join them and Paulina. "Come dance!"

I take advantage of the distraction and push myself to my feet. The room spins again but straightens itself after a second. I stumble on my way past the coffee table, but Paulina catches me and starts spinning me around to the Little Mix song Iz has playing.

It's not enough to chase the images of Becca out of my mind, but it does ease some of the tension that took up residence in my shoulders as soon as Jane said her name. I twirl around, thinking back on the last time I saw her.

After years of struggling with my sexuality in a small town, I finally started coming to terms with being bi after coming to UNS. I also made out with a lot of girls in the dorms, but nobody drove me crazy quite like Becca.

It helped that she didn't seem to notice me at all. She eats, sleeps, and breathes lacrosse, and as a freshman, I doubted I even registered as a human to her off the field. That made it easier to see her as nothing more than an off-limits crush who showed up in my head when I was in bed at night.

Or in the shower in the morning.

Or basically anytime I was alone.

Then I met my ex, Ethan, about halfway through my first year. I clicked with him in a way I never had with anyone else before. I realized I wanted something real, not a fantasy with somebody who knew my lacrosse number better than my name. I'd never even been sure I was the kind of person who could handle a relationship, but Ethan made me feel like it was possible, like we'd figure it out together.

Only I got it wrong. I got it all wrong, and when Becca was the person I bumped into after I ran out of that party so the entire team wouldn't see me sob, she knew way more than my name.

Maybe it was the few beers I'd had or just the emotional turmoil, but when I looked at her after she'd pulled me into a hug, I knew she *saw* me. I knew I saw her.

It knocked all the breath out of my body and arranged new constellations in the sky.

But the term was over. Half the campus was heading home, and one possibly-didn't-even-happen moment with Becca wasn't enough to stitch up every piece of me Ethan had ripped apart, so I went home too. I went home and patched myself up.

One step at a time. First thing's first.

"Eat wasabi! Drink some coffee!" Paulina shouts, totally butchering the words to the song. I let her keep spinning me around until the track ends, and then she, Iz, and I collapse onto the couch in a dog pile that makes Jane give us a disgruntled glare as she goes in for another piece of pizza.

"Aww, you guys, look at our little lobsters!" Paulina wiggles her foot in the air next to mine. We've all got tiny, black ink outlines of lobsters tattooed on our ankles. The whole lacrosse team has matching ones.

Why the founders of the University of Nova Scotia decided to name their athletics department after a crustacean will always be beyond me. They couldn't have picked anything more stereotypical. Seafood was one of the only things I knew about Halifax before coming to school here. The other teams in the league give us a lot of shit about our name—that is, until they get on the field with us.

Then they quickly learn some respect.

"That reminds me of Jim," Iz says. "I miss Jim."

Jim is our team mascot who gets brought out for games and special occasions. He's a six foot long inflatable lobster. Why anyone would need a six foot long inflatable lobster other than to use as a UNS team mascot, I will never know, but apparently he was found on Amazon.

"Oh my god! Jim!" I shout as I wave my foot in the air alongside Paulina's. "We need Jim!"

The whiskey is still making me get very excited about everything.

"We do!" Iz agrees. "I wonder where he lives during the summer."

"In the ocean," Jane deadpans before attacking her pizza again.

Jane is a hungry drunk.

"Probably in the athletics building somewhere," Paulina answers more logically.

"We should free him!" I sit bolt upright, making Iz and Paulina groan as I knock them aside in my sudden moment of clarity. "We must free Jim! CJ won't be mad at us if we rescue Jim and bring him to practice tomorrow."

Even in my current state, I can tell that plan makes absolutely no sense, but it sounds exciting to my whiskey-soaked brain, and it's making it much easier not to think about Becca or Ethan.

"Yes, *chica*!" Iz catches my enthusiasm and sits up too. "Free Jim! Free Jim!"

Jane rolls her eyes as I join in the chant. "Why did I waste my good whiskey on you two?"

"I think it could be fun," Paulina pipes up. "It can't be that hard to find him. He's probably with all the lacrosse stuff."

"He's probably lonely," Iz adds. "He's been by himself all summer. He needs to come home with us, Jane."

Jane is not having it. "How would you even get in the building?"

"It's only nine. I'm sure people are still in there. The gym is open twenty-four seven," Iz insists. "We could head over there now."

"Nuh-uh," Jane shakes her head. "No shenanigans."

"I mean, we *did* toast to this being a year to remember," I cut in. "Triumphantly carrying Jim onto the field for the first day of training camp would be *very* memorable. Everyone would be cheering and clapping, and Coach would be so busy calming them down he probably wouldn't even notice we were drinking last night."

The plan is starting to make more and more sense, which probably says more about my state of intoxication than the plan itself, but whatever.

"Come on!" I jump up off the couch. "Let's do it!"

Paulina and Iz follow me to the entryway so we can start pulling our shoes on, and once Jane realizes she's fully outnumbered, she grumbles her way over and agrees to 'supervise the delinquency.'

Outside, the street has grown completely dark. Patches of sidewalk are lit by the yellow glow of the streetlamps. The temperature has dropped a few degrees, but the cool air feels nice on my arms and face after the heat of the living room.

We're only a couple blocks away from campus, and Paulina freestyles her way through her modified version of Little Mix's 'Wasabi' the whole way there. I've already started to sober up by the time the athletics centre comes into view, and the dopey grin on my face has nothing to do with the whiskey.

This place is home: the grassy lawns, the old heritage buildings covered in vines, the stone pathways winding through it all, and there in front of us, the familiar shape of the glass and red brick athletics centre with a huge lobster mural spray-painted on one of its walls.

I can still remember my first time seeing it on the day of lacrosse tryouts. I've been playing since I was eleven, but as I scanned the outside of the building trying to find the spot where we were supposed to meet for tryouts, my brain kept telling me to run. Thoughts I hadn't had for years bubbled up to the surface like they'd finally reached boiling point again.

You can't take anything seriously.
This is too much for you.

You should be grateful you even got to university. You can't handle school and a sport.

You're stupid, Hope.

Then I spotted another girl carrying a lacrosse stick around at the exact same time she noticed me. She walked over and asked if I was ready to become a lobster.

And that's how I met Jane.

It only took a few minutes of talking before we realized we'd clearly been best friends in another life. It also only took a few minutes before I realized everything was going to be okay.

When I'm here with my team, everything is always okay.

"Free Jim!" Iz shouts, loping along up ahead of us in their prestigious shoes. "Free Jim!"

I can smell the freshly cut grass of the lawns around us, and I fill my lungs with a deep breath. They must have been mown today to get ready for the start of term. I always love walking around campus at night when it's warm out. It's overcast tonight, but this is my favourite place to see the stars.

We reach the building's dramatic glass foyer and follow Iz inside after they swipe their student ID. Our footsteps echo on the tile floor.

"So, uh, what do we do now?" Paulina asks in a hushed voice.

The stealing Jim plan seems extra stupid now, but it feels good just to be in the building. Everyone else is smiling too. 'It's good to be back' vibes are radiating off us like one of Jane's obscure candle scents.

"Let's walk around." I lead the way forward. "Damn, I missed this place."

I trail one of my fingertips along the wall of the hall-way. The whiskey must still be at work; because I feel like I can sense the building's heartbeat pumping along with my own. This is where the roar of a thousand crowds have cried out in victory and groaned in defeat. This is where stars have been born, where heroes have risen, where families have been forged with ties stronger than blood.

Yeah, it's definitely the whiskey.

Our shoes squeak on the fresh floor polish that's yet to be worn down by hundreds of students trudging through these halls every day of the semester. I start steering us to the lacrosse closet.

All we get is a closet. They at least gave us a bigger closet when we qualified to play for the Eastern Canada League. UNS is a well-known university, but it's not anywhere near as big or as well-funded as schools in places like Toronto or Montreal.

"Jim! I hear him calling!" Iz rushes past me as soon as the closet door comes into view. They stumble a little but make it down the hall without tripping.

I'm ready for our mission to end in defeat as I watch them reach for the door handle. A gasp bursts out of me when the knob twists and the door swings open. Iz lets out a whoop and starts doing a Backstreet Boys-style happy dance.

"Is he in there?" Paulina's Amazonian legs carry her past Jane and I, getting her to the closet in just a few steps. We jog the rest of the way to catch up.

Iz's voice filters out of the closet. "Jim! *Mi amor*! We are here to rescue you!"

When I make it over, Paulina is in the narrow closet lined with floor to ceiling metal shelves, doing her best to grab the edge of one of Jim's plastic claws where it dangles over the edge of the top shelf.

"Think tall thoughts!" Iz urges.

The tips of Paulina's fingers miss the claw by a good six

inches. "I'm gonna have to climb, you guys."

"NO!" Jane steps past me and grabs Paulina's arm. "No climbing! You do not know how well those shelves are attached to the wall."

"Paulina should boost someone!" I cut in.

"Yes!" Iz raises a hand to high five me. "Teamwork makes the dream work!"

Jane shakes her head and raises her eyes to the ceiling like she's praying for patience. "Did you two really just high five over that? It's not exactly a groundbreaking idea."

Iz and I are too busy trying to measure which one of us has longer arms to answer. I end up winning the contest, and Paulina squats down so I can scramble into a piggyback position.

"This is not where I thought this night was going," Jane grumbles as Paulina straightens up and wobbles a little before securing us both.

"You brought out the whiskey!" I accuse.

I focus my attention on Jim. To be honest, he looks pretty happy chilling up there, but we're too invested to give up now. I push on Paulina's shoulders to lift myself a little higher. She staggers underneath me but catches herself. My fingertips brush the seam of the claw for half a second, but I don't have enough grip to pull him down.

"Fuck," I hiss. "So close."

"Try again! I believe in you!" Iz calls.

A few more attempts end with the same result. I lower myself down and jump off Paulina to give her a break.

"What if you got on my shoulders?" she suggests.

"Jumping Jesus!" Jane's fisherman's wife voice is coming out in full force.

"One more try," I tell her, "and then we'll go home." I turn back to Paulina. "Uh, how do we do this?"

"I think maybe if I like, lean forward, and then Iz helps you climb onto me?"

We try a few variations of that and nearly send me crashing into the shelves, but after a few minutes of struggling, I'm settled on Paulina's shoulders. Now I'm tall enough that my head is in danger of hitting the ceiling.

"This is perfect!" I whoop. "Just move me a little closer to Jim, and we're good."

Balance is precarious up here. Paulina takes a shaky step that radiates up through my body and makes me sway from side to side, but I grab the shelves for support. One we've righted ourselves, I reach for Jim and start sliding him off the shelf.

"Look out below!"

I yank him out far enough to tip him over and pitch him down to the floor. He really is ridiculously large. Iz catches him by the tail, and one of his claws bonks Jane on the head. She backs out of the closet so she and Iz can start carrying him into the hall.

"Uh, so how do I get down?" I ask Paulina.

"Hmm. I'm not really sure."

The two of us stand there strategizing until Iz comes back in the closet.

"You guys coming?"

"I think we might be trapped in this position forever."

"Hmm." Iz crosses their arms and joins us in strategizing. We settle on a plan that involves Paulina lowering into a squat and me using the shelves and one of Iz's hands to launch myself off her.

We've commenced phase one when the sound of someone clearing their throat by the closet door catches my attention.

"Don't worry, Jane. We're—"

The words die in my throat. My whole body freezes as

the fight or flight chemicals start kicking in right along with the shock.

Becca Moore is standing in the doorway with her arms crossed, and she does not look impressed.

Iz and Paulina haven't noticed her yet, and I only realize they're still trying to get me down when Iz shouts, "One, two, three, go!"

"Wait, what am I—*Ow*! Oh, fuck."

I end up banging my forehead on a shelf, kicking Paulina in the boob, falling backwards onto Iz, and taking all three of us to the ground.

When I look up from all the groaning and limb-rubbing, Becca is still standing there in the exact same position, only now she's pressing her lips together like she's holding back a laugh.

I haven't seen her since April. She looks gorgeous, even under the building's awful fluorescent lights. Her hair is down and fanned out over her shoulders, the thick, wavy red strands making her look like she could be a siren in an Irish Spring commercial. She has a strong nose and jaw that give her a tough and commanding expression, but her perfect almond eyes and all those devastatingly adorable freckles soften them out.

I do my best to keep from doing a totally obvious full body scan, but I can't help noticing her black leggings and dark green plaid button-down. It has to be made by a company with a name like 'Lesbians R Us' or 'Wear These Clothes to Bang All the Women Ever.'

"Hey, guys," she says in a fake casual tone. The rasp in her voice makes me want to close my eyes in rapture and appreciate the sound like it's a holy choir. "How's it going?"

My throat has gone completely dry and I'm not sure

my knees are working, but Iz staggers to their feet and waves at Becca.

"Oh, hey Becca. Fancy meeting you here." They copy Becca's casual tone. "What are you doing here so late at night?"

Becca uncrosses her arms and raises a set of keys in the air, making them jingle. "I'm locking up the lacrosse closet after getting things ready for practice tomorrow. I thought maybe I could leave it unattended for two minutes."

"Ah. Well. Good thing it was us and not, like, a robber." Iz forces a chuckle.

I'm still sitting on the floor glancing between the two of them like an idiot, but Paulina has recovered enough to get to her feet too.

"You guys do know we have our first practice tomorrow at eight, right?" Becca asks.

Iz salutes her. "Aye, aye, Captain. That's, uh, why we're here. We thought it would boost morale to show up on the field with Jim tomorrow. Start training camp off right, you know?"

Becca narrows her eyes and takes a step into the closet. My heart rate climbs another notch.

"You guys are drunk, aren't you?"

To say this isn't how I wanted my first Becca encounter of the year to go is the understatement of the century. I spent a lot of time this summer visualizing how I wanted to start this semester off, thinking about who I wanted to be and how I wanted to feel. Becca usually factored in there, typically in the form of me killing it as a model lacrosse player and her giving me a quiet, almost shy compliment after practice that would lead to the two of us getting dinner and walking around the beautiful, sunset-streaked streets of Halifax like mature, responsible adults.

That's what I wanted to be this year: a mature, responsible, intelligent adult capable of serious things with serious people.

The semester hasn't even started, and I've gotten drunk the day before our first practice and tried to spirit official school property away into the night.

Once again, Ethan's voice starts clanging around in my head.

All you want to do is fuck around and blame it on everything but yourself.

"Hope?"

My eyes have gone out of focus while I stare at the floor. I look back up and find Becca watching me. Her eyes are narrowed again, but this time it's with a trace of concern.

"You okay?"

"Huh?"

She can't know I was thinking about Ethan.

"You fell," she says slowly. "Are you okay?"

"Oh. Yeah." I scramble to my feet and rub my arm. I banged my elbow pretty bad, but Becca's appearance distracted me from the worst of the pain, and it's fading now. "Um, good to...see you?"

Good to see you?

I think the fall knocked away the last of the whiskey's influence, but she's going to think I'm totally trashed if I can't start talking like a normal person.

She squeezes her lips together for a second and lets a breath out of her nose like she's holding back a laugh again. "Good to see you too, Hope. Do you guys mind getting out of the closet now?"

"Oh, I've happily been out of the closet for a while." Iz smirks as they step past me and into the hall. "Hope too. We're still working on getting Paulina over to the dark side. Jane here is a lost cause. Totally cuffed to a dude."

If I could elbow Iz in the stomach without Becca noticing, I would. We do not need to air out our dating histories in front of our captain right now.

We find Jane in the hallway with Jim lying at her feet like an oversized guard dog. She's doing her hands-on-hips, foot-tapping thing and glaring like she wishes she had the whiskey bottle to smash over our heads.

"Uh, should we put Jim back?" I ask.

"You might as well bring him to practice."

I turn around to find Becca locking up the closet door. It really is symbolic; I doubt any woman could go back in the closet with Becca and her plaid shirt around.

"And of course, you'll all be there on time and ready to play, right?"

I can't be expected to keep my crush a secret when she does things like ask if I'm 'ready to play.'

Iz gives another salute. "Yes, oh captain my captain."

Becca nods and crosses her arms. She has to know how good that makes her tits look. "Right. See you then. Goodnight."

Her eyes flick to mine, and she lifts her chin in a nod before turning and heading down the hall.

I exhale for what feels like the first time since she showed up.

"Damn!" Iz shouts once Becca's footsteps have faded. "We did it! We got Jim!"

"Woo!" Paulina raises her hands, and Iz jumps up to clap them in a double high five.

I just stand there staring at the spot where Becca disappeared around the corner while the two of them hoist Jim in the air. Jane comes over and makes a show of looking between my face and the end of the hall.

"So, Hastings, you want to tell me what's going on

there?" she asks in a voice low enough the other two won't hear.

I blink and focus on her. "Huh?"

She raises an eyebrow and waits.

"What do you mean?"

She stays silent for another moment and then shrugs. "Hmm. Guess we better get this lobster home."

The four of us hold Jim over our heads like we're the aquatic version of a Chinese dragon costume in a parade. We only make it to the edge of campus before all our arms start aching and we decide to take turns going two by two. By the time we make it to our place, the combined impact of flying today and doing four and a half shots has me ready to drag myself up to my room and pass out.

I'm about to crawl to bed after we've manoeuvred Jim inside and set him down on the couch when Jane looks up from checking a text.

"Did somebody lose their phone? It's from Becca. She says she had to get something out of the closet after we left and found a phone on the floor."

We all pat our pockets down.

"Not me," says Paulina.

"Me neither," Iz adds.

I've already felt the empty pocket of my joggers.

"That would be me."

Jane looks back down at her phone and starts typing. "I'll ask her where she is. Maybe you can go grab it."

"No, that's okay. I—"

"Whoops! Already sent it."

Great. Not only am I the drunken lobster thief, but I'm now the drunken lobster thief who can't even keep track of her phone.

Iz and Paulina say their goodnights as we wait for Becca to answer. Her text comes in about a minute later.

"Oh, she only lives a couple streets over, or she says she could bring it to practice tomorrow."

It shouldn't thrill me to find out she lives so close. Half the student body lives in this neighbourhood, but that doesn't stop my chest from doing the weird mix of constricting and flooding with warmth it does sometimes when I'm near her.

"I'll just get it tomorrow. Could you tell her thanks?"

I've done enough damage for tonight. Jane is about to send the text when I remember I actually *do* need my phone tonight.

"Oh, shit. Wait. I was supposed to call my mom when I got in. Fuck."

Jane looks up. "I'm sure she's assumed you're fine."

"Yeah..."

I could message her on Jane's phone or my laptop, but then I'd have to tell her I lost my phone within hours of arriving, and that would result in a huge conversation about whether I'm okay or not and if I'm ready to be back on campus, which is not something I feel like having at the moment.

"I should probably just go get it. What street is she on?"

Jane gives me the street name and number. We say goodnight, and I head outside. I pause on the bottom step of the stoop, take a breath deep enough to taste the salt in the air, and then take off down the street.

3

Becca

I can taste the salt in the air. I let my head drop back and close my eyes, filling my lungs as far as they'll go. Even after a few years in Halifax, I haven't gotten used to being so close to the ocean. Everything changes here. The shoreline expands and contracts like the ocean is a pair of breathing lungs too, filling and emptying again and again, over and over, always taking something when it goes and bringing something new when it returns.

Sometimes I just sit down by the water and marvel at the movement of it all. Not much moves back home in the prairies, not unless you stop and watch the ripple of the wind in the fields. The waving stalks look a bit like water too sometimes, but they're always rooted in the earth, grounded in place.

Steady.

There's nothing steady about the ocean. It sweeps in whenever it wants and rolls and rages until it decides to leave. No matter how long I stare at the waves, I can never tell if I'm fascinated or terrified.

Sometimes I think I might be both.

The echo of footsteps in the empty street makes me lift my head and open my eyes. I'm sitting on the edge of the porch that runs the length of the big heritage home me and my roommates rent the top floor of. Down at the bottom of the street, I can see a girl making her way up the sidewalk.

Hope.

I recognize the army green sweats and white t-shirt she was wearing earlier. As she gets closer, her glasses glint in the glow from a streetlamp. She's got her hands in her pockets, and the bob in her step is the picture of the phrase 'out for an evening stroll.'

She's so fucking cute.

I shouldn't think it, but I do anyway. Hope Hastings is dangerously cute. She's so cute, in fact, that the first thing I thought when I saw the phone on the floor of the supply closet was, 'I hope it's hers.' I spent way too much of my summer trying and failing not to imagine what it would be like to see her again this semester. I pictured her smile, the sound of her voice, the way her glasses sit a little crooked sometimes and always make me want to reach over to straighten them. Once in a while, I'd even get so far I'd imagine trailing my fingers from her glasses to her cheek to her lips.

I grip the edge of the porch and squeeze so hard the wood digs into the heels of my palms. She's the last person on the entire campus I should be thinking about. She's my teammate. I'm her captain. We have rules for a reason.

Good reasons. Important reasons. Reasons I can't ignore.

I push myself to my feet and head down the sunken stone slabs that lead to the sidewalk. She pauses for a second like I've startled her, and then she grins and waves before picking up her pace to meet me.

She's gotten tanned over the summer, and the teal ends of her hair suit her so well. The last time I saw her—or rather, the time before I found her trying to steal an inflatable lobster earlier tonight—she had mascara running down her face, and her whole body looked slumped and broken, like an animal curling itself into a ball to hide its wounds. I'd never seen her like that. I'd never felt the need to *protect* her like I did then, the urge so strong it was more of an instinct than a thought. Other than when she was charging around the lacrosse field—and sometimes even then—I'd never seen her do anything other than smile and laugh.

She's good at making people laugh. At team parties, she's always the first one on the dance floor. She's led her fair share of karaoke parties in the locker room. She's always moving, just like the ocean, and maybe that's why I've been fighting not to sit and stare at her the way I stare at the shoreline since the day she showed up for tryouts two years ago.

"Hey, Becca."

She stops when we've reached the same square of sidewalk.

"Hey, Hope."

A beat of silence passes. She glances at the houses around us, hands still in her pockets. I try not to look at her lips. I try not to remember how it felt to hold her that night she fell apart. It was only a hug. It's what anyone would do for a heartbroken teammate, but I don't think just anyone would be itching to hold her again even now.

"Nice street."

A laugh bursts out of me before I can stop it, the tension in me searching for a way to escape. "I don't know if I can take credit for the street, but thanks."

She shuffles her feet and lets out an embarrassed

chuckle. "Yeah. Right. I just, uh, there are some nice trees on this one. Seems like a nice place to live."

The air between us is thick with something that really shouldn't be there. I can feel it pressing in on every side of me, like insulation that blocks out the rest of the world.

"I like it," I answer. "We only moved in at the beginning of last year."

"So you have roommates?"

"Yeah. I live with Rachelle and Bailey. I guess I'll have to move again when they graduate at the end of the year. I'm doing a fifth year to finish my degree."

She did not ask for all that information, but it comes out anyway.

"Right, yeah, I remember you saying a few times last year that you've got some courses to catch up on."

I nod. "Captain duties cut into my course load a little. Protecting Jim from kidnappers is a full time job."

We both chuckle at the lame joke, and Hope glances down at the pavement again.

"Yeah, about that. We got a bit...carried away? I'm sorry. I don't want you to think that I'm—that we're not serious about the team. Lacrosse first is the Babe Cave's code of honor."

I raise my eyebrows. "The...babe cave?"

She shuffles her feet again. She's extra cute when she's embarrassed.

"Uh, yeah. Ha. That's what we call our house."

I smile at her when she looks back up at me. "I like that."

"What?" She shrugs, and her voice gets playful. "Are you telling me you guys haven't named your house?"

"I can't say that we have."

"You should consider it. I'd highly recommend the experience.'

I tilt my head. "Oh yeah? Got any suggestions?"

"Hmm." She squints and shifts her hips back and forth as she thinks. I try not to look down at them. "How about Cap's...shack?"

I make a sound between a laugh and a snort. Hope shakes her head.

"Okay, yeah, I'm terrible with rhymes. I'll workshop it."

"I don't know if Rachelle and Bailey would be down to name the house after me."

"I'd name a house after you."

The silence after she speaks seems to thicken the insulation around us. Her eyes go wide as soon as the words leave her mouth, and I can see her taking rapid breaths in through her nose.

"Right. Yeah. I am being suuuuper awkward tonight. Chatty McChatterson, as Jane would say. I should stop right now."

I want to reach out and grip her shoulder, but I keep my arms glued to my sides. "I don't think you're being awkward. I think you're..."

The only thing in this whole city that could make me consider jeopardizing everything that matters to me?

I force a chuckle. "Now I'm being awkward."

"We should make a club." She rocks back and forth on her feet as we grin at each other. "So, uh, thanks for grabbing my phone."

"Oh, shit. Right. Your phone. Let me get it. I left it on the porch."

Somehow, it took me all of two minutes to completely forget the reason she's here.

"I'll come with you. I need to see this shack."

We walk the few metres back to the house side by side. I can feel the heat of her arm just a few inches from mine. She stops for a second when I turn onto the pathway.

"Damn. You live *here*?"

The three storey historic home with big bay windows, a chimney, and a giant oak tree in the yard *is* pretty impressive.

"Just on the top floor," I answer. "It's divided into a bunch of different units that all get rented out. I don't even know how many people live in the house in total."

"Is your room at the front?"

I stop to follow her gaze up to the roof of the house, where I can see my little window covered with the lace curtains that were already there when I moved in.

"Yeah, actually. It's that one." I point it out, and she nods.

"Cute."

I need to get this phone to her fast before I do something catastrophically stupid like ask her if she wants to see the room.

Staring at her in the shadows of the streetlight, just steps away from my front door, I can't help picturing what that would be like. I'd lead her up the creaky stairs, and we'd laugh as we tried to be quiet. I'd turn the little lamp on my dresser on to keep the lighting low. She'd tell me she likes the quilt on my bed. We'd walk over to look out the window. Our arms would touch.

I'd look at her.

She'd look at me.

We wouldn't need to say anything else.

"Here." I can't meet her eyes as I thrust the phone into her hands. I feel her fingers brush mine for a second, and it's pathetic, but even that seems like it could make me gasp if I let it.

I don't know what happened that night Ethan broke up

with her, but it woke something in me that I can't put back in the dark. I'd always *noticed* her before. Anyone would. She's hot and cool and funny, and the way she moves on the field is breathtaking. It's a combination of grace and aggression I've never seen in a player before. She's triumphant.

It's never a surprise to see her score an impossible goal; all anyone can ever think when they watch her play is *of course*. *Of course* the ball went in the net. *Of course* she made that pass. *Of course* she got around the defence. Her movement seems inevitable, free from dependence on anything around her.

Just like the sea.

I always noticed her, but I never let myself want her like this. I cut myself off. I kept distance between us. I barely even spoke to her outside of practice because I knew from the second I saw her just how dangerous the pull I felt could be. I fought it for so long I could convince myself it wasn't there, but now it tugs on my limbs even when she's not around, dragging me closer to her shoreline.

"Thanks. So, uh, I'll see you tomorrow morning, yeah?"

I nod and swallow down the lump in my throat. "We hit the field at eight."

"I'll be there. Sorry again about tonight."

"Hope, it—" I falter for a second when something shifts in her face at the sound of her name. "It's okay."

She nods.

"Have a good sleep." Her lips twitch. "In your shack."

I laugh for a little too long. I'm so tense my muscles are starting to ache.

"Goodnight. See you tomorrow."

She heads back the way she came, bobbing along with

her hands in her pockets just like she did on the way here. I shouldn't stand here watching her until she's out of sight. I should turn around and head inside to close the door on all of this as I pull it shut behind me.

But I don't.

I'm still standing there long after she's gone.

———

MY ALARM GOES off at a quarter to six. The soft chimes are supposed to gradually wake me up, but my eyes fly open long before they've reached their full volume. I fumble for my phone and shut the sound off so I can lay on my back in the quiet for a moment.

The grey light outside filters through my curtains, giving my room a dim glow. The space is small, just big enough for a twin bed, a desk, and two dressers sandwiched together, but it was close to campus and fit my nearly non-existent housing budget.

The house is silent as I lay there and watch the quilt my grandma made rise and fall where it's pulled up over my chest. With so many people packed into the units, this is about the only time of day there isn't some crashing and banging coming up from the lower floors.

I stay under the warmth of the blankets for another minute before I force myself out of bed. I pass the collection of art prints I got at a Halifax craft fair and the big mirror I have propped against one of the walls to make the room look bigger as I head for the bathroom.

I have my morning routine so down pat that I'm pretty much on autopilot until I get out the door: brush teeth, drink smoothie, eat weird protein muffin thing, change into running clothes, tie shoes, grab keys, leave house.

It's an overcast morning, so there's no dramatic sunrise

to greet me, but the temperature is hovering right around perfect for a morning run. I smile to myself as I start stretching in the front yard. It's the first day of the first ever lacrosse summer training camp—the training camp Coach Jamal and I worked so hard to organize and get approval for.

When I got a scholarship from the Canadian Women in Sports Association after being accepted at UNS, I also won an annual donation to the team's funding. That's a big part of what took us from being barely more than a glorified intramurals team in my first year to where we are now: poised for a real shot at winning the ECULL women's championship this season. Just the thought has me tearing up the sidewalk at a speed way too fast to maintain for my whole run.

I know we're not playing in some huge, internationally regarded varsity league like I would have been if I'd accepted the invitation I got to go to school down in the States, but that's never stopped me from giving this team my all.

Every person on the UNS lacrosse team has their heart in the game. That means something. It shows in the way we play. It shows in the way we've performed and risen to the top. It's what gets me up before six in the morning and keeps me at the athletics centre late at night.

This team is something I can trust. It's something I can belong to and always have a place in. Sometimes it feels like the only thing I can count on, and I never want to come close to losing that again. After everything that happened in my freshman year, I've been regimenting my thoughts just like I regiment my morning routine: precise repetition with no room for mistakes.

I let my feet carry me through the sleepy streets. There are no sounds except the birds and the rumble of a few distant cars downtown. This is my favourite time of day to be outside. It feels like I'm watching the city shake off the last of its dreams, smiling down at it the way you do when you're waiting for someone you love to roll over in bed beside you and open their eyes.

The pavement under me starts to tilt into an incline as I make my way towards Citadel Hill. The city is notorious for the steep pitch of its streets, but I love the way my lungs burn as I trudge upwards. The hill makes up a park in the middle of the city that used to be an old military fort.

I wind my way along my usual route through the grass lawns, all the way to a lookout point where I can see Halifax stretched out on every side of me. To the east, it slopes down all the way to the sea. The harbour is already in action, white-sailed boats and huge cargo ships dotting the water.

A cool gust of air off the ocean lifts the ends of my ponytail. I breathe deep and smell the salt. Everything is at peace here. Everything has a place in a bigger picture that makes sense.

I'm a kinesiology major, but the courses for my minor in environmental science always make me feel like I'm standing right here on top of this hill, so high above a complicated world that it isn't complicated anymore. Studying nature in school never makes me fail to marvel at the patterns that tie us all together, the ones we move within each day without even being aware of the ways the world shapes us and we shape it.

Maybe I should switch my major.

I shake my head to push the pointless thought away, the one that still crops up from time to time. I'm too far into my degree to switch now, and my lacrosse schedule would make it too difficult to switch to a double major and still play on the team.

So kinesiology it is.

I don't want to lose the rhythm of my run, so I only pause for a few seconds before heading back down the hill. I run all the way to campus and slow to a walk outside the athletics centre. After a few laps of the lawn outside to cool down and a quick stretch, I swipe my card to get in and head for the lacrosse locker room. We share it with a few other sports teams, but it's better than having to use the ones for the student gym.

I've already claimed my usual locker for the year. I grab my backpack and gear and then head to the supply closet to grab a few things for practice. Coach will appreciate the head start. I load some pylons, jump ropes, and stretch bands into a milk crate and then shuffle my gear around so I can carry everything out to the field.

I glance up at the empty shelf that usually houses Jim the inflatable lobster, and I feel the corners of my mouth lift.

That's quickly followed by a spike in my heart rate and then a surge of guilt.

Now is not the time. It will never be the time.

I reach the field well before practice time and set the milk crate down on the close-cropped grass spray-painted with the markings of the game. Setting up the pylons is enough to distract me from Hope for a bit, and it only takes a few minutes before the same thrill of passion and purpose that sent me sprinting through the start of my run takes over again.

This is where I belong. It doesn't matter what happens anywhere else, because this field right here will always be my home.

Grab your copy here!